I0682282

THE HOME IN THE VALLEY

EMILIE F. CARLEN

From the original Swedish by
ELBERT PERCE

1st WORLD
LIBRARY
Literary Society

The Home in the Valley

Emilie F. Carlen

© 1st World Library – Literary Society, 2005
PO Box 2211
Fairfield, IA 52556
www.1stworldlibrary.org
First Edition

LCCN: 2006902692

Softcover ISBN: 1-4218-1825-6
Hardcover ISBN: 1-4218-1725-X
eBook ISBN: 1-4218-1925-2

Purchase *"The Home in the Valley"*
as a traditional bound book at:
www.1stWorldLibrary.org/purchase.asp?ISBN=1-4218-1825-6

1st World Library Literary Society is a nonprofit
organization dedicated to promoting literacy by:

- Creating a free internet library accessible from any computer worldwide.
- Hosting writing competitions and offering book publishing scholarships.

Readers interested in supporting literacy
through sponsorship, donations or
membership please contact:
literacy@1stworldlibrary.org
Check us out at: www.1stworldlibrary.ORG
and start downloading free ebooks today.

__The Home in the Valley__
contributed by Tim, Ed & Rodney
in support of
1st World Library Literary Society

TRANSLATOR'S PREFACE

A few years ago, Mrs. Carlen was comparatively unknown to readers in this country; but the marked success which followed the publication of "One Year of Wedlock" encouraged the translator in the endeavor to present that lady's works to the American public.

In her writings Mrs. Carlen exhibits a versatility which may be considered remarkable. While in one book she revels in descriptions of home-scenes and characters, in another she presents her readers with events and incidents that bear a strong resemblance to the startling and melodramatic productions of many of the modern romance writers of France.

This peculiarity, however, may be accounted for by the fact that she writes - as she herself confesses - entirely from impulse.

When her mind is clouded by sorrow - and she has been oppressed with many bitter griefs - she seeks to remove the cause of her despondency by creating a hero or heroine, afflicted like herself, and following this individual through a train of circumstances which, she imagines, would naturally occur during a life of continued gloom and sorrow.

On the other hand, when life appears bright and beautiful to her, then she tells a tale of joy; a story of domestic life, for where does pure happiness exist except at the fireside at home?

It must have been during one of these bright intervals of her life that Mrs. Carlen wrote "The Home in the Valley," for the work is a continued description of the delights of home, which, although occasionally obscured by grief, and in some instances, by folly, are rendered still more precious by their brief absence.

New York, August 15th, 1854.

CHAPTER I

THE VALLEY

In one of father La Fontaine's books, may be found a description of a lovely valley, the residence of a beautiful and modest maiden, and of the heroine of this Arcadia he writes:

"There stands our heroine, as lovely as the valley, her home, and as virtuous and good as her mother, who has devoted a lifetime to the education of her daughter."

But with the history of this maiden he weaves the workings of an evil genius, which in the end is triumphant; for even the pure are contaminated after they arrive at that period when they consider that vice has its virtues.

Our story is located near the beautiful Lake Wenner, in a valley which much resembles that described by La Fontaine. As we enter this valley, the first object that meets our view is a small red-colored cottage. A vine twines itself gracefully over one of the windows, the glass panes of which glisten through the green leaves, which slightly parted, disclose the sober visage of an ancient black cat, that is demurely looking forth upon the door yard. She has chosen a sunny spot on the window sill, for the cheering beams of the sun are as grateful to a cat, as is the genial warmth of the stove to an old man, when winter has resumed his sway upon earth. If we should enter the cottage, we would in all probability find the proprietor of the little estate seated in his old arm-chair, while his daughter-in-law

- but more of this anon.

From the cottage the ground descended in a slight slope, which terminated in a white sandy beach at the margin of the lake. Near the beach were fastened the small skiffs, which swayed to and fro amongst the rushes, where the children delighted to sail their miniature ships. From the rear of the house the little valley extended itself in undulating fields and meadows, interspersed with barren hillocks and thrifty potato patches. In the fields could be heard the tinkling of the cowbells, the bleating of lambs, and the barking of a dog as he gathered together his little flock. Carlo was a fortunate dog, for the farm was so small that he could keep his entire charge within sight at all times.

Near the centre of the valley stood a large tree, the widely spread branches of which shaded a spring, which gushed forth from beneath a huge moss-covered stone. This was the favorite place of resort of a beautiful maiden, who might be seen almost every summer evening reclining upon the moss that bordered the verge of the spring.

"There stands our heroine, as lovely as the valley, her home, and as virtuous and good as her mother, who has devoted a lifetime to the education of her daughter."

But many years before the date of our story, Nanna had lost the protection of her beloved mother; yet the loss had been partially supplied by her sister-in-law, who occupied the places of a kind mother, a gentle sister, and a faithful friend.

Nanna was now in her sixteenth year; but to all appearances she was much younger. Unlike others of her years, her cheeks did not display the bloom of maidenhood, and her countenance lacked the vivacity natural to her age. Her features wore an expression of melancholy, which was perfectly in keeping with the pallor of her cheeks, the pearly whiteness of which vied in brilliancy with the hue of a lily.

Nanna was the child of poverty, and belonged to that class of beings, who, situated between riches and nobility on the one hand, and poverty on the other, are considered as upstarts by the wealthy as well as the poor.

Nanna's father, when young, was placed in an entirely different position of life than that in which we now find him. An illegitimate son, he entered the world with a borrowed title, but with fair prospects for the future; for his father, a man of consequence and wealth, intended to marry his mother, and thus the son would bear no longer the stigma of his father's crime. But death, who in this case had been forgotten, suddenly cut the thread of his father's life, and the mother and son were driven forth from the house of their protector, deprived of honor, wealth, and station.

This is an old, very old and thread-bare story, and not more novel is that which generally follows. First comes melancholy, then great exertions on the part of the injured party; next dashed hope, and finally gloomy resignation.

The mother died, the son lived to pass through the life we have above described, but which was ended, however, by matrimony. He married after he had passed his fortieth year.

Before his marriage, Carl Lonner passed through the various gradations in society, from the nobleman to the simple gentleman. He supported himself by revenues he derived from a small business, and by drawing up legal papers for the surrounding peasantry and fishermen. For a wife he had chosen the daughter of a half pay sergeant, and in this case his fortunate star was in the ascendant, for she not only brought him a loving heart, but also the little farm on which he resided at the date of our story.

We will now, however, turn our attentions to Nanna, who is sitting beneath the tree near the spring, in which she has been bathing her feet.

* * * * *

As Nanna glanced into the clear water of the spring, she shuddered convulsively, although the air was warm, for it was a June evening, but it was a shudder from within that shook her slight form. Nanna had lately perceived that her dear sister-in-law, Magde, when she thought herself unseen, had shed tears, and the poor girl's heart beat with a sensation of undefined fear, for when Magde weeps, thought she, there must have been a great cause.

"Why is the world so formed as it is? Some flowers are so modest and little that they would be trodden under foot unless great care is taken, while others elevate their great and gaudy heads above the grass. The latter are the rich, while the little down-trodden blossoms are the poor. And so it is with even the birds! one is greater than the other, and mankind is not behind them. We belong to the poor; there," she continued, turning her deep eyes towards a distant point in the horizon, on the other side of the lake, "there lives the rich; they take no notice of us. Even the poor fishermen and peasants say, 'Our children cannot be the play-fellows of Mademoiselle Nanna.' Mademoiselle, Mademoiselle," she repeated slowly, "it is shameful to call me so! and how much better it would be to call Magde good mother, than to give her the title of My Lady! To be poor is not so bad, but to be friendless is bitter indeed."

As she thus sat, with her eyes fixed mournfully upon the distant object which was the roof of an elegant house, which was barely visible over the brow of a hill, she was startled by the noise of approaching footsteps. She had scarcely cast her mantle over her white shoulders, which she had uncovered during her ablutions, when, to her great astonishment, she discovered a stranger rapidly approaching towards her. He was clothed in a light frock coat; a knapsack was fastened upon his shoulders, and in his hand he swung a knotted stick. Nanna had never before beheld a personage who resembled the stranger. His face, browned in the sun, until it resembled that of a gipsy, wore an honest and frank expression, and his dark curling hair, which fell in thick clusters from his black felt hat, added to the pleasing aspect of his countenance.

Emilie F. Carlen

Nanna, who at her first glance at the youth, had thought him a gipsy, which wild tribe she greatly feared, was reassured by a second look.

The stranger, on his side, appeared greatly astonished at the sudden appearance of the beautiful water nymph, for such a goddess Nanna much resembled, as she stood, with her garments flowing gracefully around her slight figure; her tiny white feet playing with the moist grass, and her pale and mournful face, encircled with golden locks, that fell negligently upon her white and well rounded shoulders.

The youth thus addressed her:

"Pardon me, lovely naiad. It appears that I have taken the wrong path, although I supposed that I had chosen the right direction."

"Whither are you going?" inquired Nanna, in a voice sweet and melodious.

"To Almvik," replied the stranger.

"Alas!" said the maid, casting a peculiar glance at his knapsack, "I hoped that you were not a member of the aristocracy."

"Oh, my little sylph, for I know not what else to call you, is my face so poor a recommendation, that I cannot be considered a man because I carry a pack on my back?"

"Are those of noble birth the only men?" inquired Nanna, and a gloomy expression fell upon her lips, which a moment before had been illumined with a sunny smile.

"Ah," replied the youth, "the longer I gaze upon your dear face, the more I esteem you. Far be it from me to wound your sensitive nature. If it will comfort you, I will say that no man can long more earnestly than I do for the time when all mankind shall be equal."

"Do you speak from your heart?"

"I do, earnestly; but tell me your name."

"Nanna, Nanna of the Valley, I am called."

"That is poetical; but have you no other name?"

"I am sometimes called Mademoiselle Nanna; but that grieves me, for we are poor people."

"Ah! I thought that you were something more than a peasant girl. Pardon me, I have spoken too familiarly. I knew not your station."

"Familiarly!"

"I addressed you too warmly."

"Your words sounded well when you thus spoke."

"Possibly; but henceforth I shall address you as Mademoiselle Nanna."

"Shall we then see each other again?"

"Yes, yes, quite probably - we are to be neighbors."

"You intend, then, to reside at Almvik?"

"Yes, for a few weeks, perhaps during the whole summer; but I pray you come with me a few steps on my road, I need your guidance."

Nanna sprang to her feet, and as she stood before the young man, her eyes sparkling with unusual brilliancy, her garments falling in graceful folds over her sylph-like limbs, he gazed at her as if enchained by her almost superhuman beauty. To the youthful stranger's request she answered by putting her little white feet in such active motion, that they seemed to tread upon the air instead of the green sward.

CHAPTER II

THE COTTAGE

The interior of the little building to which we now turn, was thus arranged: The ground floor was divided into a kitchen and three other apartments, viz: - a middle sized room, by favor called the parlor, in which was generally the dwelling place of the family, and a small chamber on either side of the parlor. One of these was the bed-chamber of Carl Lonner, and the other was occupied by his eldest son and his wife.

The upper story, that is, the attic, contained two divisions, and the sole dominion of these airy apartments was granted to two younger members of the family; the front room belonging to Nanna, and the other to her brother Carl, known in the neighborhood by the nick-name of "Wiseacre," and under certain circumstances as "Crazy Carl," although it would have been difficult to find throughout the entire neighborhood a personage wiser than honest Carl.

Throughout the entire building the marks of poverty were plainly evident; but at the same time each object presented a tidy and cleanly appearance and although the cottage lacked many luxuries, still comfort seemed to reign supreme. The rush covered floor; the table, polished to brightness; and the flower vases, filled with odorous boquets of lilacs, the neat window curtains, the handicraft of Nanna, the crimson sofa curtain, embroidered by the thrifty Magde, all combined, proved that the inmates of the cottage, had not only the taste, but also the inclination to render home pleasant even under the most adverse circumstances.

* * * * *

At the time that Nanna had started forth as a guide to the youthful stranger, old Mr. Lonner was seated near the side of his bed in his private apartment. Although weighed down by age and the grief that had oppressed his early life, he nevertheless possessed that gentleness and sociability, which had ever been the characteristic traits of his life. His flowing white locks fell around his countenance, from which the traces of manly beauty had not been entirely eradicated, and as he smoked his pipe with an air of dignified pleasure, he would occasionally glance towards a young matron, who, seated in a large arm chair, was reading aloud a letter to him.

The letter bore the postmark of Goteborg, and was written by the old man's eldest son, Ragnar Lonner, the husband of the matron. He was mate of a trading vessel, and three months before had bidden farewell to his wife and family. As she continued reading the letter, three children who had been playing, commenced a little dispute about the proprietorship of a large apple. In an opposite corner Carl had stationed himself. He was a full grown youth with a face bearing an expression of mingled silliness and wisdom. - As he glanced from under his long hair, first at the bed-quilt, then at the quarrelling children, he paid close attention to all that his sister-in-law was reading aloud. Carl was not the simpleton people considered him, although his highest ambition appeared to consist in erecting dirt houses and making mud-pies.

"Magde," said the old man, casting a glance of affection upon the vivacious Magdalena. "You had better read that letter again. Ragnar is a son who has his heart in the right place."

"And a husband too!" added Magde, and a flush of joyful pride overspread her blooming cheeks.

"Yes, and a brother also; read the letter once more, it will be none the less pleasant to read it a third time when Nanna returns."

Magde, who had not refolded the letter, commenced reading again, and her voice trembled with pride and emotion as she read as follows: -

"Beloved Magde:

"When you shall break the seal of this letter, I feel assured that you will wish you possessed wings that you might be enabled to fly to your loving husband. And as I think I see you approaching me through the air, surrounded by our little angels, - may God protect them, - the tears start to my eyes, tears which no man should be ashamed to shed, and I feel an inward desire to hasten to meet you.

"But now, dear Magde, I must control my thoughts, and so direct them to you, that they shall prove intelligible. I arrived, on the eighth day of this month, at Goteborg, in safety and in good health. I hope our father is well and capable of enjoying as usual, the balmy air and bright verdure of summer.

"Our little cottage is a pleasant residence, in spite of all its disadvantages, and I feel assured that both yourself and Nanna do all that lies in your power to cheer our mutual parent, when he is sick and dispirited.

"One night while our vessel was lying in the canal, I was visited by an evil dream, but dreams are empty and meaningless, and I hope that no more of my disagreeable fancies will be realized than that you at home, may experience a little anxiety and solicitude concerning the welfare of the absent one.

"The Spring of the year is always the most severe season, for winter consumes the harvest of the preceding summer.

"Well, we have many mouths to feed - God protect our children. - When they are older they will work for us. It was my intention to send you a small sum of money in this letter; but I was obliged to wait until Jon Jonson, who is here at present with his sloop, shall commence his homeward voyage, for I can place no dependence upon young Rask to whom I am obliged to entrust this letter, as he might be tempted on his way to the post office to enter a beer-house, and there lose the money. I am forced to send Rask to the office, as I am obliged to remain on the vessel until it is unloaded.

"I will tell you in advance that I shall not be able to send you a large amount of money; but instead of that, I shall forward you when Jonson returns, a quantity of foreign goods which I have been fortunate enough to purchase and to place on board his sloop without paying the duty, which you know is heavy. It consists of sugar, coffee, tobacco, cotton yarn, and a package of silks.

"You, my dear wife, must select the best, a silk shawl which you will find in the package. Nanna may have the next best shawl, and you may give Carl the blue handkerchief which is at the bottom of the parcel. I have not forgotten father. I shall send him a small cask of liquor, and in the parcel of silks you will find a bundle of toys for the children.

"You cannot imagine - but still you must - how pleasant it is to deprive oneself of luxuries that you may provide for the wants of those whom you have left at home.

"My ship-mates frequently say that I am severe towards them when at sea, perhaps I am; but it grieves me when I see those noble men, so skillful in the management of our vessel, lavish their money when on shore in foolish pleasures. They have as great reason to be economical as I have myself, and I cannot resist from occasionally censuring them, and therefore I may not appear so kind to them as I am to you when at home, or while I am writing this letter.

Although all my efforts may be fruitless, still I feel assured that there is not one man amongst them who would not peril his existence to rescue 'the tiger,' as they call me, from any danger. They well know that I would not stop to think, but would spring into the ocean at once, if it was necessary, to rescue them.

"But, my dear Magde, a word in confidence. I am neither as wise or as well educated as my father was in his younger days, yet I would not wound your feelings either by word or action; but I must inform you that a rumor has reached my ears about a certain man, whose neck I once would have twisted willingly, because, when in church, he looked at you oftener than he did at the minister.

"But if, when I return, I discover that that villain from Almvik has been poaching on my grounds, he must look to safety. In you, Magde, I can place all confidence, and shall therefore say nothing further. And now farewell. Remember me firstly to my father, and then to my sister, and my children.

"Your faithful husband,
"RAGNAR LONNER.

"P.S. During the soft moonlight nights, when on my watch, I see your form, dear Magde, bright and beautiful, as I look over the wake of the vessel. And when the night is dark and cloudy, I see you sitting by my side, the binnacle light shining upon your pleasant face, which is illumined with smiles as I gaze upon little Conrad, whom I imagine a fine full grown lad, climbing the shrouds with all the eagerness of a competent sailor. But, belay, otherwise my letter will be under sail again."

When Magde read the portion of her husband's letter which he had intended as confidential, her voice trembled as it did when she had first read the letter.

"It would have been my desire," said she, "that Ragnar had sent the money in the letter. It has been more than three weeks, dear father, since you have partaken of other food than fish, bread and potatoes. Ah! I wish we had a quarter of beef!"

"O, stop your prating, child! Fish is very good food indeed."

"But not strengthening. How delicious it would be if we only had a partridge, or even a rabbit. Certainly they would not cost much! But who dare think of such luxuries? All delicacies must be sent to Almvik."

"God grant that we may have nothing worse to expect from Almvik, than that they should prevent us from enjoying luxuries that poor people cannot expect to procure."

"O, that is not my opinion. In winter-time, when Ragnar is at home, he procures us many a savory dish with his gun."

"Yes, but I think that if Ragnar has disturbed the hunting grounds of Almvik, he may consider himself fortunate if the proprietor has not poached upon his own premises in return. The affairs of Almvik are far differently conducted than they were formerly, under the sway of the ancient proprietor."

During their conversation the old man and Magde had taken no notice of Carl, who, while he listened to their words, contorted his face in such a manner that it would have been difficult to decide whether he was laughing or crying. He placed his hands over his face; but between his fingers his eyes could be seen peering out with a peculiar expression at Magde.

"I will no longer feign ignorance of your meaning, father," replied Magde, with a visible effort to suppress her anger. "It is true that in words, and even in actions, he has conducted himself with more presumption than he would have dared to assume last winter; but fear not, I well know how to protect the honor of my name."

"And as you thus speak you vainly endeavor to conceal your emotions," said the old man suspiciously.

"Do not think that he has endeavored to plant his snare for a simple dove. When he would snatch his prize, he may learn that I possess both beak and talons."

"Well, my child," replied Mr. Lonner, with a laugh, "it is a fortunate chance that you are the daughter of a father who was a man of the world; but your birth entitled you to a higher position in life than that which you now occupy."

"You speak strangely, father."

"Why, you might have married Mr. Trystedt who possessed riches and lands, while now you live in absolute poverty."

"Why should you think of that? Is it not better to live in poverty with love, than to possess untold riches without love? Does the whole earth contain a better husband than my Ragnar? Is he not a skillful sailor? I have no doubt but that had he not been married he would long ago have been promoted to a captaincy. He is a thousand times more of a gentleman, at any time, than that old Trystedt, who was a torment to all he whom he met."

"Thank God! If you are satisfied, then all is right, and even if we are at present in straightened circumstances all will be made right when Jonson arrives. I hope that he will be careful of the goods entrusted to him."

A slight noise in an adjoining room, notified the mother that her infant child had awakened. She instantly arose and left the apartment. Magde was a dignified and elegant woman, although her countenance was pleasing rather than beautiful, and as she moved towards the door the old man's eyes followed her with a gaze of admiration and love.

CHAPTER III

HUSBAND AND WIFE

About a half a mile from the valley - the name of which we shall conceal, as many personages who are to play a part in our little story are still living - was situated the estate of Almvik, which the present proprietor Fabian H -- , had purchased one year before, and had immediately removed thither with his family.

Mr. H --, and above all his puissant wife Mistress Ulrica Eugenia, her proper name, but which she had afterwards tortured into the more refined patronymic, Ulrique Eugenie - were individuals who moved in the higher classes of society, at least he who should endeavor to prove to the contrary would find the task a thankless one.

Mr. Fabian H --, imagined himself a second Brutus, that is to say; he was fully convinced that the time would certainly arrive when he should arouse himself from his present listlessness; when he should be released from the thraldom of his wife, and awaken to renewed strength and vigor. But it was much to be feared that poor Brutus never would realize his bright anticipations of liberty.

Mistress Ulrica Eugenia was characterized by a strong desire to assist in the work of emancipating women from the tyranny of men, and that she might forward the good work she had entirely set at naught the command that a wife should obey her husband; she openly declared that the ancient law which compelled the woman to subserve to the man, was but a concoction of man himself, that the Bible itself never contained such an absurd command, but that the translators, who she triumphantly affirmed were men, had placed that law in the scripture, merely to suit their own selfish ends. She also affirmed that she would stake her life upon the issue that she would not find, even if she should search the scriptures through, such an absurd command. And she was right. *She* would not find it.

In the immediate neighborhood of Almvik, Mr. H -- was reverenced as a wealthy nobleman, and a man of power. He wished to be considered a hospitable man, and frequently rejoiced his neighbors with invitations to visit his beautiful estate. To him strangers were godsends. He entertained them to the best of his ability, invited the neighbors to see them, and although his little soirees were very pleasant, still, as the guests were drawn from all classes of society, many amusing scenes were enacted, in all of which, Mistress Ulrica Eugenia performed a prominent and independent part.

Although Mrs. Ulrica had liberated herself from all obedience to her legal master, and had in fact assumed the reins of government herself, she nevertheless possessed some, if not a great deal of affection for the rosy cheeks and sleepy eyes of her husband, and at the same time she kept a watchful eye upon those whom she suspected of partaking with her in this sentiment. Not only was Mrs. H -- occasionally aggravated by the pangs of jealousy, but she was also tormented by the thought that her husband entirely confided in her own fidelity, thus at once cutting off the possibility of a love quarrel and a reconciliation.

Upon the evening when we first made the personal acquaintance of the inmates of Almvik, Mr. H -- and his wife were riding out in their gig; for in the morning they rode in a light hunting wagon, and at noon they used the large family coach.

Mr. H --, immediately before starting forth on the ride had received a severe lecture from his spouse, because he indulged in an afternoon's nap, instead of devising means for the amusement of the family, that is, of the worthy dame herself, and their only treasure, the little Eugene Ulrich, and Mr. H -- , we say, never felt inclined for sprightly conversation after such a lecture.

He well knew that he would be obliged to succumb in everything; but like a stubborn boy, who is punished by being compelled to stand in a corner until shame forces him to submit, Mr. H -- determined, to speak figuratively - to stand silently in that corner the entire day rather than to acknowledge himself conquered.

That was, at least, one point gained, towards his emancipation. It cannot but be supposed, however, that, if the lecture had been upon any other subject less trivial than the mere act of sleeping, Mr. H -- would have undoubtedly acted in an entirely different manner. At least that is the only excuse we can find for his conduct on this occasion.

"Well," said Mistress Ulrica, straightening herself up in her seat with the utmost dignity, "upon my honor, Mr. H --, you are a *very* agreeable companion."

"I am obliged to be careful while driving."

"Is it necessary that you should sit there as dumb as a fence post?"

No reply.

"Well, I must say that your sulkiness is not to be envied. Suppose some one should see us - I mean you - why they would readily believe that your wife was an old woman."

"Now, now, my dear Ulrique Eugenie, don't - "

"Your dear Ulrique Eugenie is not yet thirty eight years old, and even though you are two years younger, I do not think that should make any difference."

"On the contrary, on the contrary," grumbled her husband, chuckling inwardly.

"I do not know but what your words have a double meaning; but Fabian, *we* must not quarrel, let us become reconciled, there is my hand."

"Your heart ever overflows with the milk of human kindness, my dear," said he.

"Thank you, my dear husband, - but can you imagine what I really intended to say?"

"Indeed I cannot."

"I intended to say, should you ever cast your eyes upon another - "

"God forbid!"

"You may well say God forbid, am I not your wife, who will not allow her rights to be trodden under foot?"

"Am I not aware of that?"

"Even if you are, my dear, there is no harm in my saying that if I should discover the slightest cause which would arouse my suspicion I would scratch out your eyes!"

"Sweet *Ulgenie*!"

Ulgenie, a word which the reader will observe, is compounded from the words Ulrica and Eugenie, was one of those contorted terms of endearment, which Mrs. H -- permitted her husband to use during their moments of tenderness. Should he wish to address her in an extremely affectionate manner, he would term her his "pet Ulte," an expression which had also originated in the fertile mind of the loving wife!

On this occasion the husband considered the first expression sufficiently affectionate, and in all probability many tender recollections were associated with those three syllables, for no sooner had he uttered the name "Ulgenie," than she cast her eyes downward with an unusual gentle expression, and in a changed tone of voice, she whispered: -

"Never again my dearest husband shall we differ in our opinions. Equality in marriage renders it a useful institution; but to change the subject, it is long since you have made any hunting excursions, dear Fabian, to-morrow you must go."

As Mistress Ulrica was determined that her husband should become a skillful sportsman, she gave him rest neither night nor day, unless he devoted at least two days of the week to hunting or fishing excursions. Not that Mr. H -- was a sportsman; but that it afforded his wife great pleasure to inform her guests, that a certain moorcock was killed by her dear Fabian, or that he had caught the pike which then graced their table, for, she would add complacently, her Fabian was well aware that she took great delight in eating the game taken by his skillful hand.

Therefore there were no means of escape for him, he must by force become a sportsman, for a wife who is laboring for the emancipation of womankind, never will permit her desires to remain ungratified. During the conversation the vehicle approached the mansion. Mr. Fabian H --, during the entire ride, had thought upon the pipe and sofa which awaited him upon his return, for he smoked like a Turk, and loved the ease of oriental life. There was one pursuit, however, which afforded him still greater pleasure, and that was to ogle other men's wives, for he was an unfortunate son of Adam, never being able to discover beauties which his wife might have possessed.

* * * * *

"Who can that be!" exclaimed Mistress Ulrica Eugenia as the gig entered the court-yard, "who is that elegant young man descending the door steps? is it possible that he is my nephew little Gottlieb?"

"Yes he is, my dear Aunt Ulrica, I was little Gottlieb, but I have grown up to be big Gottlieb," answered a cheerful voice, and the next moment the young man whose acquaintance we have before made, embraced the lady warmly, and then heartily shook his uncle's extended hand. Uncle Fabian however, was not overjoyed at his wife's determination of introducing into his house a stripling who might perhaps become a spy upon his actions and make reports that would call forth the entire vigor of his wife's tongue.

After the first torrent of welcomings, questions and answers, - for Mr. H -- did not dare do otherwise than to cordially welcome his guest - had subsided, and the family had entered the dining room, and the hostess had pressed the acceptance of a third cup of tea upon the young man, who was already sufficiently heated without undergoing this ordeal; she thus addressed him: -

"Now, my dear little Gottlieb, you look remarkably well, you little rogue. Is it really true that you have made this long journey to see us on foot?"

"It is indeed true; this green coat is my usual costume when I do not wear a blouse, which is my favorite garment. My better apparel is contained within my knapsack, and thus I have given you an invoice of my wardrobe, which you see, my dear aunt, is not very extensive."

"But your under-clothes, my child?"

"What, under-clothes, do you think I could give my dear uncle so much trouble as to bring linen clothes with me?"

"What a careless fellow you are!"

26   Emilie F. Carlen

"'You have now,' said my mother, when I took my leave, 'you have now four rare pieces of linen, styled shirts; but when you return, you must travel by steam, for you will undoubtedly possess twenty-four!'"

"Ah!" replied his aunt, with a smile, "I understand you now."

"How do you understand me?" inquired Gottlieb.

"As belonging to that class of persons, sir, who never find themselves at a loss," replied uncle Fabian, in a tone of voice which he intended should be overwhelming.

Gottlieb, however, was not inclined to be thus easily driven from the field. "You have hit the nail upon the head," said he, with an assumed expression of respect for the decision of his uncle, "and it is by the means of that very trait of character which you have mentioned, that I hope to work myself through the world, although I am only the son of a poor secretary in a government office, who is embarrassed by debt and a large family, thus you perceive I cannot depend solely upon the whims of fortune."

"What then are your prospects for the future?" inquired the lady seriously.

"I have but one," replied Gottlieb.

"And what is that?"

"My plan is very simple, I have thoroughly studied financial matters, and in the fall intend to help my father in his office, so that he can spare the services of his two assistants. He will then have only one salary to pay; but I think that I can do the work of three, and as I intend to become a model of order, capability and energy, I hope to be able to win the favor of the head of the treasury department, so that when my father, who at present is in a very feeble state of health, shall be obliged to resign, I may be appointed in his stead. This is my plan."

"You are a shrewd young man," said Mistress Ulrica.

"It is not necessary to be shrewd when the high road is plain before you."

"But at least you must possess sufficient knowledge of the world to prevent you, in your youth, from leaving the high road, and wasting your time in useless dreaming."

"Of dreaming, he who has nothing but his head and hands to depend on, must not be afraid. If one wishes to enjoy pleasant dreams, he must not trouble his head about that which he is to eat when he awakes."

"Good! good!" exclaimed Ulrica, "I hope that your wise plans will succeed, and I do not doubt but what they will, they are so well laid, and aside from that you are not striving for yourself alone, but for your parents, to whom I am sure you will always prove a dutiful and grateful child."

"That is why I should become my father's successor, dear aunt. Had I not thought of this plan, I would undoubtedly have formed some other; but with this I am satisfied."

"And do you intend to afford us the pleasure of your company this summer?" inquired uncle Fabian, abruptly.

"With your permission, dear uncle, your invitation arrived at a lucky moment, as it came during my vacation."

"Well, well, nephew," said Mrs. Ulrica, "we will go and prepare a chamber for you."

"Nephew, nephew," exclaimed Gottlieb, merrily, "why we look more like cousins!"

"You are a little wag!"

"O, I must say more. My mother might have been your

mother also, from all appearances."

"Ah, I was a mere girl when she was married. She was the eldest while I was the youngest of the family, and the fourteen years discrepancy between our ages accounts for the differences in our appearance."

"And riches and fortune also," added Gottlieb; "poor mother, misfortune has always been her lot; and although she has much trouble, she has nevertheless an angel's forbearance."

"Her disposition resembles mine more than her person does," said Mrs. H --, casting a glance of tender inquiry upon her husband.

"Yes, my dear," replied he, "your angelic disposition and patience are well known."

He well understood the smile with which his wife had accompanied her words.

"Good Fabian, you know how to appreciate your wife!"

"Sweet Ulgenie!"

Gottlieb glanced from his aunt to his uncle.

"Strange people these," thought he. "I think they are playing bo-peep with each other, or perhaps they are blinding me; well, I care not; so long as they do not disturb me, I will not meddle with their affairs."

CHAPTER IV

THE ATTIC-ROOMS

As we have before stated, Nanna had supreme control over one of the attic-rooms of the cottage, and for a long time it had been a sanctuary in which she stored her precious things.

Old Mr. Lonner loved Nanna as the apple of his eye. She was not only the youngest child, and consequently the favorite, but she also possessed strong perceptive qualities, and a heart susceptible of the tenderest emotions. She was, so to speak, a living emblem of those harmonious dreams that her father in his youth had hoped to see realized.

The pale and delicate countenance of Nanna, who he thought was destined in all probability to droop and die like a water lily, which she so much resembled, carried the old man's mind back to the time when his father had promised to wed his mother, and he sighed as he thought how different Nanna's station in life would have been had that promise been fulfilled. Instead of neglect and insult, homage from all would have been her portion.

Yet Nanna was the pride and joy of her father's heart, for Ragnar, who at an early age was obliged to labor for his own support, had preferred to become a sailor, rather than to acquire a refined education, and Carl could scarcely comprehend more than that which was necessary for the performance of family worship. Nanna, on the contrary, would listen to her father with the utmost pleasure and interest as he related and explained matters and things which were entirely novel to one placed in her position of life.

And then, with what eagerness would Nanna read those few books with which her father's little library was supplied! She fully comprehended all she read, and she could not resist from becoming gently interested in the characters described in her books. She sympathised with the unhappy and oppressed, and although she rejoiced with those happy heroes and heroines who had passed safely through the ordeals of their loves, yet when she read of the fortunate conclusion of all their troubles, she would sigh deeply.

But after sighing for those who *had* lived, she sighed also for the *living*.

She looked forward, with terror, to the day when she should lose her father, whom she worshipped almost as a supreme being.

Her innocent heart shrunk within her as she thought of the time when a man, - for these thoughts had already entered her little head - should look into her eyes in search of a wife. Who shall that man be? she thought. Is it possible that he can be any other than a peasant or a fisherman? Perhaps he may be even worse; a common day-laborer of the parish.

O, that would be impossible!

Such a rude uncouth husband would prove her death. How could she entertain the same thoughts, after her marriage with such a boor, as she had before? He could never sympathise with her. No, she would be obliged to remain unmarried for ever. Perhaps not even a laborer would wed her! On St. John's eve, when she had ventured to attend the ball, did any body request her to dance? No, not one, no, they only gazed at Mademoiselle Nanna, with a stupid and imbecile stare - *she* did not belong to their class.

* * * * *

The next evening after Nanna had encountered the young stranger near the spring, she was seated alone in her bedchamber. During the entire day she had endeavored to assist her sister-in law, in the various domestic duties, with her usual activity; which however it must be confessed, was mingled with much pensive abstraction. But after the tea service was removed, she had retired to her chamber, that she might in solitude commune with her own thoughts.

The silence of her apartment was soothing to Nanna's mind.

Besides a small sofa, which was her sleeping place, her little dominions contained a book shelf; three or four flower vases; a bureau, and a small work table. The two latter articles of furniture were specimens of Carl's workmanship.

Carl, when he *chose* to display his ability, was a skillful carpenter, and formerly Nanna was his special favorite. Of late, however, it could readily be perceived that Magde possessed his affections. She, had she so chosen, could have abused him as if he had been a dog, and like a cur he would have crept back to kiss the hand which had maltreated him. Magde, however, was soft-hearted, and did not abuse her power over the singular boy; but she compelled him to labor with much more assiduity than he had formerly. When at home, Carl generally performed the duties of a nursery maid. The children remained with him willingly, for he tenderly loved them; in fact every child in the neighborhood loved the "Wiseacre," for he would play with them, and upon all occasions take them under his special protection. When he saw his little nephews and nieces, subjected to the discipline of their mother, he would fly into a frenzy of passion, and then he was called, "Crazy Carl." He was an inveterate enemy to corporeal punishment, and he could invent no better method of explaining his doctrine, than by administering to those, who differed with him, a practical illustration of the cruelty of personal castigation. Therefore he would fly around among the

Emilie F. Carlen

parents and the straggling children, preventing their punishment of his favorites by means of his own stalwart arm, and then after the tumult had subsided he would repent and tearfully sue for pardon.

Crazy Carl was laughed at for his exertions in behalf of the children, yet to spare his feelings the necessary punishment of the children was deferred till he was out of sight. None of the neighboring peasant women would leave their homes, to go to the market, to a wedding, or to a funeral, without requesting Carl to remain with the children, and upon his compliance they would go forth untroubled, for they were well aware of the unbounded influence "Wiseacre" possessed over the young people.

Carl's bed-room, which adjoined Nanna's apartment, contained a bedstead, a well whittled table, and a chair mutilated in a like manner. In this chair Carl would rock backward and forward, for hours, and with half closed eyes would look as if by stealth, at a striped woolen waistcoat, which was suspended against the wall, or some other little gift from Magde.

At the same time that Nanna was seated in her room looking towards the large tree near the spring, Carl was rocking in his chair, gazing with his peculiar expression at a brown earthen vase, which was standing upon the table before him. The vase contained two freshly plucked lilacs, one blue and the other white, which emitted a fragrant odor. After Carl had sufficiently regarded these objects, he slowly jerked his chair towards the table, and at each pause his mouth widened into a simple simper. At length he arrived so near the table that by bending forward he could have easily touched the flowers with his nostrils. To accomplish this movement, which was his evident intention, he proceeded with as much gravity and carefulness as he had evinced in approaching the table. He bowed down his head inch by inch, until he could no longer withstand the desire of his senses. With one plunge he thrust his nostrils amidst the fresh leaves of the fragrant flowers.

Suddenly, however, he raised his head, a thought struck his mind - his face lengthened and his brow became cloudy.

And yet a few moments ago he appeared supremely happy.

*   *   *   *   *

Nanna's pretty face was pressed against the window pane. Her little world had never before appeared so fresh and beautiful. So great was her abstraction that she did not hear the door open, as Carl with his peculiar lofty strides entered the room.

"Thank you, Nanna," said Carl. Nanna did not hear him. His voice was lost in her recollection of the words of the strange youth, she had met the day before.

"Thank you, Nanna," repeated Carl.

Nanna started. "What for?" said she.

"Do you not know?" replied Carl, "why for the flowers!"

"Flowers?"

"O," said Carl smiling imbecilely and gazing vacantly around the room.

"If you found lilacs in your room, I did not place them there," said Nanna.

"Ah! then perhaps little Christine sent them to me."

"No, dear Carl," replied Nanna, "the flowers were sent by one who is better than even myself or Christine."

"Who can it be?"

"Magde, of course."

"Ah!" Carl slowly stepped towards the door. "Magde, yes, I ought to have known that!"

"Ask her, and then you will know certainly," said Nanna.

"O, no, but they are beautiful flowers. I hope I will not break them, they smell so sweetly!"

Thus saying Carl strode across the floor to his own chamber where he again seated himself upon his chair and resumed his former occupation; but he did not profane them with his nostrils, for now he regarded them in a holier light. They were Magde's gift.

While he was thus happily engaged, a messenger arrived at the cottage to disturb him. A peasant's wife, who wished to attend a funeral desired his services, and the obliging Carl, although he protested that he had a great deal to engage his attention at home, willingly promised to go to the woman's cottage and take care of her children until her return. In order that his arrival at the cottage might be joyfully welcomed, he returned to his room, and commenced the manufacture of sundry whistles and as he whittled and sung verses of his own composition - for Carl was a poet - he occasionally cast loving glances towards the brown earthen vase.

But how was Nanna employed? Was she reading some of her favorite books, an amusement to which she often devoted her leisure hours? or perhaps she was proceeding over the path which conducted to the spring in the meadow. Neither. She at present appeared perfectly satisfied with her unaccustomed listlessness, from which however she was soon aroused.

From between the trees that bordered the side of the hill, she saw a green coat emerge, which when it reached the plain made its way towards the little fountain beneath the tree.

The wearer of the coat, who was the young man who had carried the knapsack and had called Nanna his little naiad, a term which he supposed she did not understand, cast himself upon the grass near the trunk of the tree. Perhaps he was expecting some one.

For a few moments Nanna stood undecidedly upon the threshold of the door. Her inclinations drew her towards the spring; but her modesty cautioned her to remain.

Why had she so long postponed her usual walk on this particular occasion? She had not expected any one. Certainly not!

At length, however, she seized her bonnet and hastened from the room.

CHAPTER V

THE FIRST DISAPPOINTMENT

Nanna had arrived at the bottom step of the flight of stairs, when she encountered Magde who was returning from a visit at a neighbor's house. She had walked fast, and her face was crimson with heat and vexation. When Magde first saw the young girl, she drew her bonnet close around her face, intending to enter the house as quickly as Nanna wished to depart; but when Nanna had reached the threshold she exclaimed:

"Where are you going?"

"To take a little walk," replied Nanna.

"Be careful, Nanna," said Magde seriously, "you will soon be a young woman."

"And why should that affect you so?" replied Nanna, astonished at Magde's caution.

"O, only that poor women who wish to preserve their fair fame, are not allowed to go out when they choose."

"What did you say?"

"I say that the sun, earth, water, trees, and flowers, are made only for the rich, who can admire them from their fine carriages and pleasure yachts."

"But, dear Magde, you have always - "

"Silence, child," interrupted Magde, "you do not know the insults to which we females of humble birth are exposed."

"We are not born that we should thus be insulted," said Nanna.

"True, true; but then we should have been born as deformed and ugly as those sins, which even our modesty will not preserve us from being suspected of."

"Can that be possible!" thought Nanna. Magde, who as she spoke had passed her hand upon her forehead, now removed it, and from the expression of her dark eyes, which beamed with her accustomed cheerfulness, and from her proud and lofty bearing, it could be perceived that she had regained her usual self-possession.

"I grieve you, dear Nanna," said she in a softened tone of voice, "I do not imagine you to be more than a dove which is still fostered within the dovecote. But I was troubled, as I am sometimes, without really knowing the cause."

"Is there no cause, then?" inquired Nanna.

"I can say that there is or is not a cause, and therefore shall remain silent."

"Then remain silent, dear Magde, let us speak no further on the subject," said Nanna quickly, for she was burning with impatience to visit the spring.

She longed to discover by experience whether it was really so dangerous for a woman to walk out alone.

Until the day before, it had not been dangerous, for no one

had forbidden her the free enjoyment of God's beautiful earth, and neither had her modesty ever been insulted. On any other occasion, Nanna would have been influenced not only by curiosity, but by a far purer feeling, namely, sympathy for Magde's sorrows, - for she dearly loved her sister-in-law, - and would have asked an explanation of matters which she at present was anxious to avoid.

Magde was silent.

Nanna stepped over the door sill.

But stern fate compelled her to turn back a second time, for the moment that Magde turned to pass into the house, old Mr. Lonner advanced to the door.

"Nanna my child," said he, "bring my chair out into the dooryard. The evening air is so cool and pleasant that it will invigorate my old body; but it would be better I think, if my rheumatism will permit it, to take a little stroll in the fields, with the aid of my walking cane on one side, and with you as a staff to support me on the other."

Nanna blushed so deeply that she felt the blood burning her cheeks, as she advanced the opinion that the exercise might prove injurious to him.

"Poor child, you are grieved on account of your old father. I will take your advice. Bring my arm-chair out, and we will sit here and have a little chat together."

Hitherto, when her father had chatted to her of all that he had seen and experienced, Nanna had considered herself amply rewarded for her days of labor, but on this occasion, she not only went after the chair reluctantly, but also, when she as usual seated herself with her knitting work on her little bench at his side she sighed deeply. Her father did not observe her dejection, perhaps he considered it an impossibility for his precious jewel to sigh when she was with him.

"Well, Nanna," said he stroking his long beard which gave a venerable appearance to his benevolent features, "are you thinking of the fine shawl that Ragnar is to send you by his friend Jon Jonson?"

"Not at all, dear father," replied Nanna.

"True," continued the old man, "your disposition in that respect does not resemble Magde's. She is pleased, as every young woman should be, when she has an opportunity of decorating her person with elegant clothing."

"I think, that hereafter," said Nanna, slightly confused, "I shall also cultivate a taste for such things; but thus far I have had but little opportunity."

"I hope so," replied her father, "I have frequently been much troubled in mind, when I have observed your indifference to dress, so unnatural to one of your age; but which is only a result of the romantic notions that you have always indulged in."

"But dear father, is it not wrong to strive to make ourselves beautiful when we are only poor people?"

"Beautiful!" exclaimed the old man, "what put that into your little head?"

"Magde told me that all poor women ought to be born ugly, that their reputation might not be suspected."

"Magde was a little out of humor, when she said that, and she who wishes to please her husband so much, could not have really intended what she said."

"Yes, but when a woman is married, it alters the case entirely."

"But why should not an unmarried girl wish herself handsome for the sake of her father, her brother, and above all for her own sake? That is a good wish so long as it continues innocent."

"When then, is it not innocent?" inquired Nanna.

"It is no longer innocent when the love of fine apparel, and the desire to be beautiful, changes the heart, and the girl neglects her duties, and gives her sole attention to that which should only serve as a simple recreation; but that I am sure will never be the case with you."

Nanna was silent. She drooped her head. "There is no danger of that," thought she, "for who will care to witness the change?"

"On next St. John's day," continued her father, "you must wear that elegant silk shawl which belonged to your poor mother."

As Nanna heard these words, a smile of peculiar meaning passed over her lips. It was the smile of a woman who anticipates a future triumph.

"Thank God," said the old man, turning the conversation in another channel, "for all the blessings he has bestowed upon us. Although we may now be in trouble, when Ragnar's packages arrive, we shall be in better circumstances. Poverty has many blessings of which the rich man cannot even dream. The poor man's gratitude and joy for even the slightest piece of fortune is too great to describe. The rich man has not that relish for the good things of life that the poor man has."

While honest Lonner was thus losing himself in his meditations, Nanna moved in her seat uneasily, and dropped stitch after stitch of her knitting-work. The former topic of conversation was endurable, but this -

Meanwhile, however, she did not dare to express her desire to be liberated from her irksome position. Why was she afraid to do so? She asked herself the question; the only reply she could make was, that yesterday it would have been easy for her to say, "Father, I want to take a little walk in the meadow;" but to-day, oh! that was different!

"I see you have your bonnet on!" said her father, "were you about taking a walk?"

"I have not been out of the house before, to-day," replied Nanna.

"Well, then run away, my child; take all the enjoyment you can. You have but little here."

Perhaps it was by expressions of this description from her father, that mournful thoughts were engendered within the mind of the young girl, causing her to fancy that something was wanting to complete her happiness, and that she stood beyond the pale of those who should have been her companions.

It is certainly plausible to suppose that these moments which the old man had set apart for familiar conversation with his daughter, whom he loved above all earthly things, for she reminded him of past days, might have proved highly detrimental to Nanna's sensitive and susceptible mind.

As matters now stood, it was plainly evident that, however economical, industrious and thrifty she might be, Nanna would be compelled to be content with her lot, should she wed an honest mechanic or a sloop captain, which were the highest prizes which she, or any of the neighboring maidens, might expect to win.

Like a captive bird which, after many fruitless struggles, finally regains its liberty, Nanna quickly made use of her restored freedom, and hastened from the door-yard. She was fully convinced that the young man was no longer in the meadow, and now she suddenly remembered that she had said nothing to her father or Magde about the stranger whom she had encountered the previous evening. How strange it was that she had forgotten to tell them! Yes, it was the strangest thing that ever had occurred during her whole life, and how greatly astonished they would be when she should tell them of her little adventure! Thus thought Nanna, as she proceeded towards the meadow.

CHAPTER VI

THE AGREEMENT

"It was just as I thought!" exclaimed our heroine, as she looked, with pouting lips at the reflection of her pretty figure in the clear waters of the spring. Never before had her hair been so nicely arranged, and her neat white apron, which she had kept concealed beneath her cloak during her entire conversation with Magde and her father, and which she had carefully tied about her waist as soon as she had entered the meadows, how pretty it looked! But how was she repaid for all her trouble? She was about disencumbering herself both of her apron and a little scarf which she had thrown over her shoulders, when she heard a voice that she had already learned to distinguish, calling to her in the distance.

With pleased astonishment she lifted her eyes, and saw an individual whom we need scarcely inform our readers was the owner of the knapsack. He was descending a hill, holding to his lips a blade of grass, upon which he would occasionally blow a vigorous and ear-piercing blast.

"Have you come at last, my naiad queen?" said the youth. "We were such pleasant companions last evening, that I came hither in the hope of finding you at your bath again."

"A naiad queen might bathe her feet before you; but I - " She ceased speaking, and a deep blush suffused her cheeks.

"Ah! then you know something about the naiads, my child?"

"Yes, and about the sylphs, too," replied Nanna, nodding her head, proud at having an opportunity of displaying her knowledge before one whom, besides her father, was the only person that she had ever cared to interest.

"You surprise me! What have you read?"

"O, a little of everything. My father has a large book case, and I have a small collection of books, myself."

"Hm, hm," said the embryo secretary, "but enumerate to me some of the books you have read."

"Do you really wish to know?"

"Yes, dear Nanna, - pardon me - Mademoiselle Nanna I should have said. Now Mademoiselle, please be seated, the grass is quite soft. I wish to catechise you a little."

"But I shall not answer you, sir, if you call me Mademoiselle; it sounds so cold and disagreeable."

"Well, I will be careful not to do so; but let us make a commencement."

"With my qualifications?"

"Certainly; but why do you sit at such a distance?"

"We are not so far from each other."

"That proves you to be no mathematician. Now, tell me, how many yards distance are there between us?"

"Three, I think."

"Poor child, you have not reached your A B C's in arithmetic;

but I will be your instructor."

"How so?"

"You shall soon see." He quickly unloosed his neckcloth. "This," he continued, "is precisely one yard in length. Now, I will measure the ground, and when I have measured three yards, then - "

"What then?"

"Then I will seat myself; for you have yourself chosen the distance."

The unsuspecting Nanna had not the slightest idea of the little plot the young man had arranged to entrap her. The poor child was unaccustomed to mirth; for although Magde, Ragnar, and Carl, often indulged in boisterous sports, still Nanna never could feel an inclination to mingle with them, but had merely smiled at their ridiculous jokes. Never had the clear ringing laugh of gleeful childhood issued over her lips; but upon the present occasion her innocent heart entered into the spirit of her gay companion, and when he deliberately measured three lengths of his neckcloth from the spot where he was sitting, and then gravely seated himself at her very side, a merry laugh broke from her lips, in which the youth joined.

"Well," said he, assuming a comfortable position, "I can touch you, at least, now."

"Yes," replied Nanna seriously, for she was musing on Magde's words of caution, "yes, you can; but I do not wish you to."

"You do not?"

"I do not," replied she firmly.

"What an obstinate little creature you are!"

"You desired to know what I have read," said Nanna, wishing to change the subject of conversation.

"True, but why do you hide your little hand under your apron, I shall not touch it without your permission?"

Nanna smiled as she slowly withdrew her hands from their place of concealment and folded them upon her lap.

"Now, my child," said the young man with an assumed air of dignity, "first of all, you may commence at the beginning."

"When I was a little girl, my father bought for me some picture books, which as I read, he explained to me. Next as I progressed further - "

"Well, what happened?"

"Next I studied the catechism, which I liked very much, then I commenced reading the bible, a book which I love above all others, the new testament especially. All that I do not understand my father explains to me, and after he has finished, I go alone to my room, and as I read I cannot refrain from weeping - But my tears are not sorrowful, I think only of - "

"Of what?"

"I know not whether I should tell you that."

"Certainly you should; am I not your friend?"

"Well then - but do not speak about it to any one - I cannot help thinking that if I had lived when our Saviour was upon earth, I should have been one of the holy women."

"Who ever heard of such ambition! Why perhaps you would like to have been the virgin Mary, herself?"

"Oh," exclaimed Nanna, turning her face, that she might

conceal the blush, which his words of ridicule, as she esteemed them, had called forth.

"But, my child," continued her companion, "we will dwell no longer upon your holy thoughts, so different from others of your age; proceed if you please."

"Aside from the books I have mentioned, at my father's request, I studied history, geography, natural philosophy, and finally ancient mythology."

"You surprise me! Your education has not been neglected; but you can write, can you not?"

"Certainly, and I have also practised drawing a little."

"Indeed! upon my honor, Mademoiselle Nanna you frighten me!"

"Why?"

"Because I cannot comprehend how you can use all your knowledge in this valley."

"I have often thought of that," replied Nanna, sighing deeply.

"Perhaps, it is not such a terrible matter after all," said Gottlieb, "I must thoroughly convince myself."

Gottlieb now commenced to examine and cross-question Nanna in the various departments of learning that she had mentioned, and was pleased to discover by her accurate replies that she comprehended thoroughly all that she had studied. In fact, Nanna was quite his equal in her knowledge of Ancient Mythology, which had always been her favorite study.

"But how is it possible that your father should be so well educated?

Yesterday, when we were walking together, you told me that he had resided in this valley nearly half his lifetime, with scarcely sufficient means to support himself and family."

"Alas! a sorrowful story is connected with my father's younger days; but he never speaks of it. He had high hopes, when young, and had they been realized, he would have been a man of consequence; but the death of his patron crushed everything."

"I must call upon your father some pleasant evening. Do you think he would be pleased to see me?"

"Of course, and Magde would also."

"Your sister-in-law? Well, well, I will soon visit them both; but listen now - "

"I will."

"As the error has already been committed - "

"What error?"

"That you should have been taught more than you ought to know; but still, it is now too late to repent as you have already learned a little, and I do not think there will be any harm in teaching you more."

"Who will teach me?"

"I shall of course. - I have an idea."

Nanna glanced inquiringly towards her companion. "You might be able," he continued, "to earn a little competency for yourself; would you be willing to become a school-teacher?"

"O, yes, nothing could be better! Then I would not be obliged to think of - of - "

"Of marriage?"

"Yes, of marriage."

"And I am of your opinion, for to speak candidly, whom could you marry?"

"I do not know; there is the parish tailor, who has already spoken to Magde about it - "

"The parish tailor! - Aha!"

"And Captain Larsson who owns a sloop, offered Ragnar two barrels of rye flour if he would speak a good word to me about him."

"Two barrels of rye flour as a bribe! And your brother's reply?"

"O, Ragnar is not to be played with," replied Nanna; "'if you wish to purchase my sister,' said he, 'you had better speak to her yourself, she has not authorized me to sell her.'"

"So you have two lovers!"

"Yes, and the sexton, an old widower, is the third. He has considerable wealth, and therefore applied to my father, himself."

"Without success?"

"Yes, father told him I was too young."

"Do you not prefer either of your suitors?"

"I would rather throw myself into lake Wenner, than to marry either of them."

"Then let us speak of the school. It will give you a little income, and is, as far as I can see, the only method of using your accomplishments to advantage."

"You are right. It is my only choice."

"I fear so too, for a lover suitable for you would not in all probability find his way hither; but in me you have found a friend at least."

"Thank God, for that."

"But it is necessary that we should make one agreement - "

"What is it?"

"That we shall not fall in love with each other."

"Oh, there is no danger!"

"Ah! who can be sure of that? You possess beauties beyond your personal charms, Miss Nanna, that may conquer me in spite of myself."

"You are also beautiful; but I do not believe that - that - "

"You do not believe that you would ever fall in love with me, you were about saying. Upon my word that is so much the better, for to speak truly I am placed in as bad circumstances as you are yourself."

"You are!"

"Yes, yes, I speak the truth. My only ambition is to become an assistant in my father's office."

"If that is the case," said Nanna, "you must fall in love with a rich girl only."

"I shall be careful of my own interests I assure you," replied Gottlieb, "but now this perplexing point is rightly settled - is it not?"

"Yes, you are to marry a wealthy girl, and I am to keep a school, is that the agreement?"

"Yes, and now we must make another arrangement, which is that we must agree to meet each other during the evening hours at this spot. I own many books that will be useful to you, and if you can sing - "

"I can sing a little, and the old sexton says my voice is beautiful."

"Allow me to hear you sing."

"To-morrow, I cannot this evening."

"O, you should not refuse a friend in that manner. It would be quite different if I was your lover."

Without further words, Nanna commenced singing an old ballad, and her sweet voice, as she trilled forth the beautiful words of her song, fell upon the ear of her young companion like the soft music of a bird.

"You sing excellently, Nanna, and I think your voice would be improved if you could play upon the guitar. I have one at home, and might bring it with me."

"But the guitar would not benefit my future pupils."

"It will serve for your amusement after your scholars have left you in the afternoon. You will find such a relaxation quite necessary, and when you play upon it, and sing one of your beautiful ballads, you will think of your friend."

"And drive away the tedium of the long hours. - O, sir, you are too kind!"

"Stop, Nanna! Call me Gottlieb, not sir. You know friends should - "

"Thanks, Sir Gottlieb! What a beautiful name! But it is quite late!"

Nanna, who was fearful that Magde, anxious at her long absence, would come in search of her, arose from her seat upon the grass, and hastily departed.

CHAPTER VII

THE CHASE

The next morning, a few hours before Carl, whistling a ballad of which he was the author, commenced his journey over ditches and stiles, to fulfill his engagement to watch with the children of the peasant woman, Mr. Fabian H -- was awakened by his affectionate wife, who informed him that it was time for him to prepare himself for his hunting expedition.

Sleepy, and unwilling to leave his cozy bed, for the sake of enjoying the damp morning air, Mr. Fabian addressed his spouse with all the tenderness which his state of mind would permit:

"Dear Ulgenie, you - "

Mistress Ulrica, however, did not permit herself to be moved by this gentle epithet.

"Fabian," said she, shaking his shoulder roughly, "you are going to sleep again. Quick! get up! I have had your top boots nicely greased, and on the chair you will find your hunting coat and game-bag. Everything is made as comfortable as possible."

"Sweet Ulgenie," expostulated Mr. Fabian.

The amiable lady smiled as she heard him speak, and had not

an unfortunate yawn accompanied those two tender words, in all probability they would have terminated this chapter. But the word yawn is not found in Love's dictionary, and consequently the unlucky husband was forced to rise from his bed preparatory to going forth to perform deeds of valor in obedience to the commands of his mistress.

"Do not neglect to awaken Gottlieb. He also must learn the noble art of hunting."

"I will, my dear, I will," said her husband, perspiring with his exertions, as he forced himself into his hunting garments which Mistress Ulrica had made from a pattern of her own invention. But when Mr. Fabian had completed his toilette, he hastened from the house, intentionally forgetting to awaken Gottlieb, for, as we shall soon discover, he had urgent reasons for wishing to perform his hunting exploits without the hindrance of a companion. As Sir Fabian was, so to speak, his wife's butler, he had provided himself with a deputy butler, who generally received a hint of the day and the hour, when stern fate would compel his master to encase his feet in heavy hunting boots.

We now see this martyr to the holy cause of matrimony, puffing and blowing beneath the weight of his heavy gun, as he wends his way across the fields towards a certain spot in the forest at which he finally arrives. He looks around him with searching eyes; his brow is clouded with anxiety and impatience. Suddenly his eyes gleam with an expression of joy; but he instantly recovers himself and assumes an air of dignified composure, while he gazes angrily upon the form of a man, who is approaching him through the trees.

"Fool! you have kept me waiting!" said he harshly as the man advanced.

Humbly but with a humility which was more assumed than natural, the "Butler," presented Mr. Fabian with two hares, and two partridges; which would fill his game-bag uncommonly well and ensure a loving welcome upon his return home. After this ceremony was performed Mr. H -- threw his accomplice a few pieces of silver, and when the last named performer in this little scene had vanished, our huntsman fatigued by his arduous exertions cast himself upon a moss-covered bank and was soon continuing the dream which had been so unpleasantly interrupted by his sweet Ulgenie.

*　*　*　*　*

"In the woods, near the sea I have lived
Many a day!
Ho, ho, ho,
Ha, ha, ha,
It is so lovely on the earth!"

Thus sang or hummed Carl as he proceeded on his way.

Suddenly he experienced a strong desire to rush into the woods to listen to the sighing of the wind as it swept through the high branches of the trees. In this music Carl took such delight that he would listen to it, for hours, while great tears of pleasure and excitement would roll down his sun-burnt cheeks. But it was the pleasure and excitement of a religious enthusiast in the house of the God he worshipped. Carl never spoke of these sentiments, and how would it have been possible for him to do so. He never thought from whence they originated. He followed his inclination only.

While Carl was thus engaged he suddenly saw an object which caused him instantly to neglect the sound of his favorite music. In the grass near the fence over which Carl was about climbing, he saw the slumbering huntsman, with the freshly killed game reposing at his side.

Carl, without knowing why, had conceived the idea that Magde disliked Mr. Fabian H --, and as for himself, he instinctively hated that worthy gentleman. And another thought entered his head as he looked upon the game. He remembered that Magde had once said: "Ah! had we but a hare or a partridge, how delicious it would be! But such things are too good for us, they must be sent to the manor house."

Carl laughed silently. He extended his hand towards the sleeping man, and then withdrew it undecidedly. Our friend Carl possessed a few indistinct ideas concerning the law of *meum and teum*. By dint of great exertion, his father had implanted in his mind the great necessity of observing the eighth commandment, and upon the present occasion the lesson of his younger days interfered in a great degree with the accomplishment of his present designs; for as he gazed upon the objects of his envy, he muttered to himself:

"*The Eighth Commandment:* Thou shalt not steal!"

His brain was not only troubled with the eighth, but the words of the tenth commandment came to his memory, "Thou shalt not covet thy neighbor's wife, nor his servant, nor his maid, nor his ox, nor his ass."

As he thus spoke, and thought first of the commandments and then of Magde, he continued to advance and retreat, wavering in his decision, and he might have remained in this state until Mr. Fabian awoke, had not a bright idea forced itself upon his mind.

"O," exclaimed he, "the commandments say nothing about *game!*" and as even the veriest simpleton has it in his power to convince himself of the purity of an action, however wrong, Carl soon satisfied himself with the excuse which he had so ingeniously invented. He entirely forgot the closing line of the commandment, "nor anything that is his," which, however, would not bear consideration on that occasion. He therefore seized the two hares that were nearest him, and by the assistance of a long stick he gained possession of the partridges also.

In the meantime, Mr. Fabian's assistant, who had not yet left the forest, having been attracted by Carl's movements, had been an eye-witness to his proceedings. But instead of warning the lad of his crime, the spectator seemed rather to rejoice at his patron's misfortune. He might safely do this, for after the crime had been committed, he could easily disclose the name of the thief, and thus avert suspicion from himself. He thought that Mr. H -- would not injure a person of Carl's character, and that at all events he would be likely to receive a proper reward for any zeal he should exert to promote the interest of his employer. Carl had discovered that his actions had been observed; but as the spectator, by sundry winks and nods, seemed rather to encourage than to prevent him, Carl proceeded without fear.

And now, having won the victory, he hastened to Magde.

But here trouble awaited him.

When Carl presented Magde the game, she was delighted; but after her outburst of admiration had subsided, her first question naturally was as to where he had procured his prize.

"Is it not enough that it is here?" said Carl, as he stood on the threshold, twirling his hat in his hand.

"Heavens! I trust you have not procured it in an unlawful way?"

"No, I got it while going the right way," replied Carl, mischievously.

"My dear Carl," said Magde, seriously, "you must not think to deceive me by your cunning words."

"You should not say so," answered Carl, sulkily.

"No, I should not, Carl, I spoke foolishly; but if you are a good boy, and love me, you will tell me who has given you this game, or whether you have promised to pay for it by working by-and-bye."

"I have already worked for it," said Carl, with a laugh, "but I must go now, or else I will be too late at Sunnangaarden."

Thus saying, Carl was about putting his long legs in active motion, when Magde exclaimed:

"Carl! Carl! a word more! stop, Carl!"

"I have staid too long already," said Carl; but still he remained.

"Tell me frankly, Carl, did you procure the game honestly?"

Carl, who rested upon the tenth commandment, in which neither hares nor partridges were mentioned, answered shrewdly:

"If you doubt my honor, I will refer you to the catechism. Do you believe in the catechism?"

"Is it true then that you have done nothing contrary to its precepts?"

"It is indeed true," replied Carl, gravely.

"Then I am satisfied," said Magde, "and I am grateful to you, my good Carl, for the welcome present."

"Good? Yes, can I really believe you, Magde?"

"Yes, I so consider you, and therefore I am good to you."

Carl commenced laughing, and assumed a crane-like position, as he balanced himself upon one leg. This was his usual custom when pleased.

"Well, well, then you love poor Carl a little. That's good!"

"Carl is my good boy," replied Magde, who during the conversation had been engaged in spreading out a number of skeins of knitting yarn that had been placed out to bleach upon the grass plot.

"Listen," said Carl, approaching nigher to Magde, "would Magde shed a tear upon my grave if God should call me from earth?"

There reposed in these words a tone of mingled fear and humility, and Magde, much moved by the peculiar expression of Carl's countenance, replied:

"Certainly, Carl, I would shed many, many tears, for I believe there are none who love you as I do."

"I am grateful, Magde," said Carl, violently scraping the ground with the sole of his hob-nailed shoe, an action which could scarcely be called a bow - "your words shall be remembered. I am Magde's servant, and shall be so as long as I live."

With these words, he turned on his heel, and trotted towards his place of destination.

"The poor lad has a good heart," thought Magde, as she concluded her labors in the yard; but she little imagined the true state of Carl's heart.

Magde now entered the house to prepare breakfast. Her three children crowded around her, loudly testifying their admiration of the partridges and hares. She commenced dressing the game with that placidity of countenance, and with that dexterity which proved she was well versed in that most important branch of a housekeeper's duties - cookery.

CHAPTER VIII

CONCERNING THE HUNTER IN THE WOODS, AND HIS HOMEWARD WALK

We now return to our friend the sportsman, who soon awoke from his sound slumber, quite refreshed. He yawned, stretched himself, and mechanically extended his hand towards the spot where he had placed his game-bag.

Although his hand touched nothing but the grass and his gun, he nevertheless was not troubled, for he thought that he had miscalculated the distance. He searched still further; but to his surprise the game-bag was still missing. He now raised himself up in a sitting posture, and rubbing his eyes vigorously, he searched the ground closely. But his eyes, usually so good, must have been dimmed by some enchantment, for he could perceive neither the hares nor the partridges, which he could not but think were there.

Determined, however, not to believe in such marvels, for honest Fabian was a man of intelligence, he arose and peered through the bushes in the grass; he looked in the air, and he closely scanned the tops of the trees; but his efforts were fruitless. The game was not to be found.

"It is astonishing!" said he to himself. "I can not believe it! They must be here! But where the devil are they then!"

The trees retained a stubborn silence, and their example was followed by the earth, the air, and the water. Although the heat of the day was rendered still more insufferable by Mr. Fabian's thick hunting suit, yet his flesh chilled with fear when he discovered the actual loss of his partridges and hares.

To return home without his game, was a misfortune, which under ordinary circumstances he could have endured; but on this occasion he had reason to expect a more than usually severe lecture from his wife whose command he had stubbornly disobeyed by not awakening Gottlieb. While the unfortunate sportsman was bewailing his fate he discovered the face of his "butler," who was peering out from between the bushes with an expression of mingled humility and mirthfulness.

"Where are my partridges, you rascal?" shouted Mr. Fabian, his face glowing with anger.

"Do you think, Mr. H - - , that I have taken them?"

"Such a jest would be but natural. What are you doing here? Have I not paid you enough?"

"I never do anything without orders, and if you do not wish me to remain, I will go instantly. I thought, however, that you would be pleased if I should tell you what had become of your game."

"That is just what I wish to know! Has any one presumed to steal it?"

"Very likely."

"Who? Quick! Tell me!"

But the butler answered only with a long drawn. "Ah!"

"Can you substantiate what you are about to say?"

"I can swear to it, if it is necessary. I waited here only that I might be able to explain everything to my employer, after he should awake."

"You are a fine fellow, now tell me what evil being has entered the woods, and committed this depredation?"

"If you wish to have a full account of the matter, you should tender full payment," said the butler, who considered this play of words exceedingly apt and forcible.

"Yes, yes, I will not be ungenerous," replied Mr. Fabian taking a bank-note from his pocket.

"Carl, - the fool of the valley - purloined the hares and partridges."

"What! that cur! - the son of old Lonner!"

"The same."

"Are you certain?"

"Yes, as certain as I am that I live."

"Good," said Mr. Fabian, and he repeated the same word several times, each time appearing better satisfied, and certainly the thoughts that occupied his mind must have afforded him great pleasure, for he not only forgot the trouble that awaited his return home, but also the question, which in truth should have been the first one - why the Butler had not stopped the thief and rescued the booty. The Butler, however, thought it expedient not to await further questions, and therefore soon found an opportunity of retreating.

Our readers may be assured that when the sportsman returned home his wife was not in the best of humor. She awaited his coming in the parlor; but when she heard his footsteps in the court-yard, she could no longer restrain her impatience, but hastened to the window and exclaimed:

"Where were your silly thoughts wandering, when you left the house without calling Gottlieb. I must say that you conduct yourself friendly towards *my* relations, and I do think it is equally astonishing that you have come home without him. I sent him to look for you a long time ago. What! can I believe my eyes! Where is the game that I was to have for dinner?"

"Dear Ulrique Eugenie, can you not wait until I have changed my clothes? I have travelled so far through the woods, that I can scarcely breathe, I am so weary."

"Where is the game?"

"Whew!" ejaculated her husband, "I can stand these clothes no longer." Thus saying, he hastened into the house, and proceeded to his apartment.

But this respite was of short duration. Mistress Ulrica Eugenie was familiar with the road to the chamber, and her rage reached its highest point, when she heard that the game which was intended for her dinner, had been stolen while her husband, overcome by his arduous exertions, had fallen asleep.

"O, if I only knew who did this, yes, if I only knew, I would have the rascal put in the stocks. But you, you dormouse, yes you, you call yourself a man! you! Don't you wish to borrow my petticoat! To sleep when engaged in the noble art of hunting! To complain of fatigue! Fie upon such men! But can you not discover the thief?"

"No, my dear, I assure you. I cannot, how could I know what happened while I was sleeping?"

"That is the reason why you never knew anything in your life," replied the exasperated woman. "But see there comes Gottlieb with a partridge in his hand. He is a pattern. *He* never allows *his* game to be stolen," and Mistress Ulrica composed her features, and assumed an expression of motherly benevolence, while she descended the stairs to receive her nephew.

"Thank you, good Gottlieb," said she meeting him at the door, "thank you, your uncle has been unfortunate this morning; but come with me to the dairy, and you shall have the cream of an entire pan of milk."

"The milk also, if you please, aunty, I feel myself able to devour every thing, pan and all."

"Well, satisfy yourself. By and by we will go to my bleachery and you may select a piece of linen. - Do you understand?"

"Not a word. It is all a mystery. But I do know that there is not a nephew on the entire Scandinavian peninsula, who possesses an aunt with such an affectionate disposition."

"Ah, you flatterer, it is well that you are my nephew or else Fabian might be jealous."

"Well I am not sure but that he may yet have an occasion, for, I am not aware that nephews are forbidden to love their aunts."

From that day forward Gottlieb was taken under the especial protection of his aunt, and as her favorite he was certain of a comfortable and pleasant life. When she became acquainted with his manners, virtues and accomplishments, her esteem for him was, if possible, doubly increased.

What could he not do, the dear boy? Not to speak of his wonderful success in amusing little Jean Ulrick, Mr. Fabian's sole heir, he was able to read aloud to his aunt from her favorite volume, and to repeat with almost sublime patience, all those tender passages to which she in a plaintive tone would sigh *de capo*. More than all this. He could sing - the model nephew - and accompany his voice with the guitar not only to the tune of "my love and I," but also to his aunt's favorite ballad, "In the shadows of the wood; in the cavern hid away." And finally there was not a female domestic in the house who dared to compete with Gottlieb in the art of chopping string beans. In short, he was a nephew whose peer could not be found in all Sweden, and who knows whether the piece of linen he chose from the bleachery was the last he received from his indulgent aunt.

Poor Gottlieb, while you are thus the prime favorite of your strong minded aunt, having free access to the pantries and dairy-rooms, have you no misgivings that the day will arrive when the doors of this house shall be closed against you? Relentless fate who ever demands a sacrifice. How true are the words of the wise Solomon, "All is vanity and vexation of spirit; and there is no profit under the sun." But it is not to be believed that Mr. Fabian's slumbers were disturbed because his wife had deserted him. No, he even preferred the company of hunger and thirst rather than that of his Ulgenie. Not that this state of mind originated from the many lectures he had received from his wife. Ah, no, there were far more powerful reasons; but it is certain that if Mistress Ulrica had suspected that her husband's indifference arose from any other motive than the wish to escape a deserved punishment she would have, undoubtedly, increased the vigor of her tongue to such a pitch that his house would have been uncomfortably warm to him.

After dining upon Gottlieb's partridge which had done much to smoothe her ruffled temper, Mrs. Ulrica was thus insinuatingly addressed by her husband:

"Have you any errands for me to perform at the parsonage, dear Ulgenie? I wish to ride down there to talk over the parish matters with the parson."

"That's right, dear Fabian. Take Gottlieb along with you. He would like to see the young ladies, each of whom are worth a ton of gold."

At this proposal Mr. Fabian's brow darkened; but the gloom was soon dispelled as Gottlieb declined the pleasure of going, and the first smile which the young man had received from his uncle was when he replied: "Excuse me to-day, my dear aunt, I wish to write to my mother."

He had no desire to disappoint his young pupil of the valley.

"Excellent youth!" exclaimed his aunt, "pleasure cannot wile you from your duties. God forbid that I should attempt to do so; and you Fabian," she added extending her arms towards her husband, "kiss me before you go. Your Ulgenie has no desire to deprive you of any reasonable enjoyments."

CHAPTER IX

MR. FABIAN AND MAGDE LONNER

"O, how thankful I am that you can come out here on the green, dear father." Thus said Magde, as she gave old Mr. Lonner his hat and cane, after Nanna had filled and lighted his pipe.

It was a beautiful scene to behold the two sisters thus employed. Ragnar was right. Without waiting for a request, they were apparently striving to outvie each other in performing little services for the old man. In short, Mr. Lonner had not a wish which was not gratified. They anticipated his every desire.

"There, that will do, my daughters; I thank you. I feel so young to-day, that I am quite happy. My rheumatism has left me almost entirely; so give me your arm, Nanna, and we will go."

"Where are you going?" inquired Magde.

"O, after we have taken a short walk," replied Nanna, "I have proposed that we should go to the spring in the meadow, and sit down awhile. It used to be one of papa's favorite spots."

"Perhaps you had better take a book with you," said Magde, "and then you can read to him."

Nanna blushed. Her object was to afford to her father another and much greater pleasure. She hoped in this manner to introduce Gottlieb to him before the youth should visit the cottage, because she feared that Magde in that case would wonder at her familiarity with the new comer.

Many times during the day, Nanna had endeavored to say to Magde, "last evening, and the evening before, I met an elegant young man near the spring in the meadow;" but for some unknown reason, the words never passed over her lips. She imagined that if she was alone with her father, she would not fear to tell him, and she also thought that when Gottlieb would see her with the old man, he would know that she had not agreed to meet him alone.

Her father would also converse with them about the time when she should commence her school, about which she had already erected many castles in the air. A little house she had thought should be erected in the valley. Here she should dwell alone with her cat, her little goldfinch with his elegant green cage, and she would also have a shed for her cow. She also wished to take a dog with her; but finally she thought she would not do so, for he would eat too much, and aside from that, would not be of the slightest benefit to her, for Carl would certainly assume the entire control of him.

There was no doubt, she had thought, but that good Carl would help her with her heavy work. That is, he would come to her little house on Wednesday and Sunday afternoons, to scrub her floors and bring the wood, while she was engaged in making cakes and pies for her father and Magde, who should visit her on those evenings. Of course this plan was to be followed during the summer only. During the winter, she would spend those afternoons and evenings in the large house.

What true happiness did the girl experience as she thus innocently dreamed of her future life! Her joy was increased as she fancied herself seated in her little school-room after the close of her labors for the day. That little room was to be a bright place in her memory forever for was it not he, her friend, who had told her that she would require some recreation after school hours, and was he not also to teach her the means for doing so?

We will not describe Nanna's blushing confusion as she told her father of her acquaintance with Gottlieb, neither will we paint at length, the mingled sentiments of fear and hope which filled the old man's heart as he heard his daughter's story; but will simply remark that the meeting between old Mr. Lonner and Gottlieb was mutually gratifying, and that as is naturally the case under such circumstances, they each wished to continue the acquaintance thus pleasingly commenced.

Upon the sand in front of the cottage Magde's children were playing in the sun, while Christine, the servant girl, was dividing her attention between her sewing work, and the baby which was reposing in a kneading trough, upon a little bed of rushes. She would also occasionally cast her eyes towards the other children, as they dug little ditches which they filled with water brought from the house in an old kettle, and then sailed their little bark boats in these miniature canals.

In the meantime, Magde, as usual, was sitting in the parlor, weaving at her loom with such violence that the window panes rattled in their sashes. As she was thus engaged she hummed a little song, which Ragnar during their courtship had frequently sung beneath her window as a signal that he wished to see her alone. As Magde loved her husband above all other earthly things, his favorite song had never become discordant to her. This song she took most pleasure in singing when she was alone, for then she could give full rein to her fancy, and look forward to the time when her loved husband should become a captain, and command an elegant schooner in which he could receive his wife, for she hoped that she might be able to take one voyage at least to Goteborg, to preside at the table in Captain Ragnar's cabin.

Then thought she, what a great stir her appearance in the

vessel would create! "Heavens," one would say, "what a beautiful wife our captain has!" Yes, the captain is a man of taste. "The captain, always the captain. O, how grand it sounded! The captain loves her so much," the sailors would also say, "that he scarcely takes his eyes from her, and how affectionately she looks at him! O, it must be a happy life, to be thus married!"

While Magde was thus engaged in her pleasant reveries, the latch was lifted and the door swung open slowly.

"Mercy! What can be Mr. H -- 's business here!" she exclaimed.

"O, do not disturb yourself," said Mr. Fabian, for it was our valorous huntsman who thus disturbed Magde's dreams, "I hope everything may be arranged without trouble. I am not the man who would injure his neighbor, even if I had it in my power."

"What do you mean!" exclaimed Magde dropping her shuttle in her terror.

In the meantime the worthy gentleman had gradually approached Magde, but so softly and cautiously that he resembled a cat about pouncing upon a trembling mouse.

"Heaven forbid," replied Mr. Fabian, "that I should think that you knew anything about it. A woman so virtuous as you are, would not engage in any wrong action; but I do think that a man's property should be respected."

"Mr. H --, if you have any evil tidings speak them out at once. Perhaps Jon Jonson has arrived, and the goods that Ragnar - "

"With a deep blush Magde suddenly ceased speaking; but her visitor required nothing further. He pretended, however, not to have understood her words; but as he well knew that Jon Jonson's vessel was still at Goteborg for he expected some merchandise in it himself, it did not require much penetration for him to surmise that the mate Lonner had taken an opportunity of sending home some smuggled goods by his friend Jonson.

"I know nothing about Jon Jonson's vessel," said Mr. H -- after a moment's pause, "but, I can readily perceive that you expect some compliments from your husband."

"Yes, not only compliments; but also a quantity of merchandise," replied Magde, who, after a moment's reflection had concluded that it was better not to make a secret of it, "as Ragnar had a little overplus he concluded to send us a few necessary articles from Goteborg. We are poor, and cannot demand credit until he returns."

"It is better not to do so," replied her visitor, "but at present we have neither Jon Jonson nor Ragnar to speak about. A certain person in this neighborhood has placed himself in an unpleasant position."

"Who can it be?" exclaimed Magde, terrified by Mr. Fabian's imposing aspect, "I will run and call father!"

"If the old man is not at home," replied her visitor concealing his joy by assuming a frown of vexation, "it will be better not to call him as it will only cause the venerable man much pain."

"Tell me, do tell me, what has been done?" stammered the frightened woman.

"I refer to your brother Carl!"

"Carl, the half-witted Carl."

"O, he is in no want of wit, and his weak mind shall not serve him as a protection when he stands before the justice. Theft is theft, no matter who commits it. At least so the law considers it."

"The game!" cried Magde clasping her hands in despair and terror.

"You are right, the game that he stole from me this morning while I was sleeping. I knew full well that the proud and conscientious Magde, would not deny that he had brought it home."

"But who could have - have - "

"Right, who could have believed that he would have done so, and that is the very point, and an unlucky one, for it proves that he must have been seen while committing the theft."

"How terrible this is! A few days ago I happened to say that I wished we had some game for our old father, and now - now - "

"Calm yourself," interrupted Mr. Fabian, extending his hand and enforcing his consolation by a love-tap upon Magde's shoulder. In her affliction Magde did not withdraw from this salute, and Mr. Fabian had an opportunity of gazing upon her lovely neck for a full moment, to prolong which he would have given the value of a hundred hares and partridges. But Magde arousing herself from her stupor, looked her guest full in the face, and there read an expression which displeased her.

With a blush she replaced the handkerchief around her neck, and suddenly enquired:

"What then, sir, is the real intention of your visit? You said you would not disturb us, and as the game is untouched we can return it immediately."

"The game is not the object of my visit."

"What is then?"

"The theft. Carl will be brought before the justice, I told you there was a witness to his crime."

"But how can that happen unless you enter a complaint?"

"Have I not the right to enforce the law which is made to protect our property? but it is possible that I might hush the matter up if I chose; and when I fancy that I see the poor fellow under arrest, when I behold him in the culprit's box, in the court-room; when I - "

"May God protect him!" interrupted Magde, "you have said enough, Mr. H -- . I am but the wife of a poor sailor; but if my humble prayers will be of the least avail - " and Magde, the proud Magde, who before had often dismissed Mr. Fabian with disdainful gestures, now clasped her hands, and looked into his face with an expression of tearful entreaty.

"O, do not despair, my dear Magde," said he, "such tender prayers and looks, have a wonderful influence upon me. Aside from that your present attitude is perfectly charming."

Overpowered by a sudden revulsion of feelings, Magde closed her eyes, and sank her head upon her bosom.

"I see," said she, "that you do not intend to assist us from our present trouble."

"On the contrary," replied Mr. Fabian with much animation, "I will do everything for you, if you will only conduct yourself towards me, in a manner different from that which you have done heretofore."

"If Mr. H -- demands nothing more than friendship," replied Magde, with difficulty repressing her anger, "that shall not be wanting."

"Nothing more, upon my honor," said Mr. H --, joyfully, "if you, dear Magde, will promise that when you meet me you will favor me with a look of kindness, I assure you by my honor, that nothing more shall be heard about this unpleasant affair; and as a proof that we shall hereafter be friends, I demand the slight favor of a kiss."

"That cannot be," replied Magde, with the coolness of despair, "I love Carl as my brother, and will give anything to preserve him from disgrace, except that which does not belong to me."

"What do you mean, my little piece of stubbornness, do not your lips belong to yourself?"

"From the moment that I entered my bridal chamber, I considered myself as belonging to my husband alone, and Mr. H --, you can be assured that you are not the person who can cause me to forget my husband's rights."

"Look you," shouted a harsh voice from the door, "before Magde should kiss your wrinkled old lips, I would run into the prison of my own accord;" and first Carl's head, and then his uncouth form appeared, as he entered the room. His face was convulsed with passion, and his eyes glanced irefully upon the surprised Fabian.

"Simpleton! you trespass upon my good nature!" exclaimed Mr. Fabian, foaming with rage.

"Do I?" replied Carl, "perhaps I shall trespass upon something else. Do you know, sir, what I shall say when the justice questions me?"

"What would you say, good Carl?" inquired Magde, encouragingly.

"I would say, for I know exactly how it will come to pass, I would humbly say to the justice, that I did take the hares and partridges from the proprietor of Almvik."

"Yes," interrupted Mr. Fabian, "you will be obliged to show your hand."

"'Now,' the judge will reply," continued Carl, without noticing the interruption, "'My lad, why did you do so?' Then I will answer, because it is not forbidden in my catechism; if the game had been an ox or an ass, I would not have taken it. Then I would say to the justice, at the same time looking at him in this way" - and Carl made such a ridiculous grimace that Magde nearly laughed outright - "that there was no danger that Mr. Fabian H -- would frighten such fierce animals as the ox and the ass, for it is his custom to charm the hares and partridges by the sweet sound of his snores, for your Honor must know that this huntsman pursues his game while comfortably snoring in the grass."

"What do you say, clown?"

"And then I can call as a witness the very man whom you intend to use against me, and finally I think that the justice will smile a little when I tell him that Mr. Fabian H -- was willing to forget all harsh measures for a kiss from Magde."

"Ha! ha! ha!" exclaimed Mr. Fabian, with a forced laugh, with which he attempted to conceal his uneasiness, "you are a waggish rogue! Your last words have afforded me so much amusement that I have not the heart to injure you for such a trifle. But listen, you little simpleton; you must not suppose that the justice would allow you to say all that. No, he would have sent you away long before you could have had time to utter a word about it."

Carl made no further reply than by applying his thumb to his nasal organ; and gyrating his fingers in a manner so significant that we will not endeavor to interpret his meaning. Having executed this manoeuver, he hastily left the room, but remained at such a distance that he could keep a watchful eye through the open door upon the unwelcome guest.

Mr. Fabian, who did not wish to appear vanquished, was at a loss how to change the conversation to such a theme as would afford him a suitable opportunity to take his leave in a dignified manner. But good Magde, who had now entirely recovered her usual equanimity, soon assisted him - by means of that instinct which sometimes puts superior knowledge to the blush - out of his dilemma by saying:

"I am grateful to you, Mr. H --, for having forgiven Carl because his words amused you; but what a simpleton the boy is!"

"It was because he was a simpleton that I forgave him; but now as my visit is at an end, I will release you from your unwelcome guest. As for the game, Carl can keep it. It would at all events create suspicion if it was sent to Almvik."

"And you, Mr. H --, you will not be angry with us?"

"I, God forbid. When I forgive I forget everything."

Magde arose and courtesied as her visitor took his departure. She accompanied him a short distance from the house, and waited till he unfastened the horse's halter.

After mounting his animal, he drove his horse near the spot where Magde was standing, and as he passed her he bowed deeply, but his face wore an expression that caused her entire form to tremble with an undefined fear.

CHAPTER X

THE TRUANT

Fourteen days elapsed. Gottlieb had fully learned the road from Almvik to the cottage in the valley. It had never entered the mind of any one of the inmates of the cottage to consider him a dangerous guest. Magde, who possessed a quick eye, soon discovered that Nanna was the cause of his visits; but she also perceived that Gottlieb was no dissembler. Magde did not look further than this, for she did not suppose Nanna would ever love one who did not return her affection. Unrequited love she did not believe in, and she thought that Nanna was of her opinion in this respect.

And in truth thus it appeared, for neither Nanna nor Gottlieb experienced the slightest degree of restraint when in each other's society. The change that had taken place in Nanna's appearance was marvellous; the blossoms of buoyant and happy girlhood had usurped the place formerly occupied by lilies on her cheeks, and our young hero had more than once laughingly said:

"It is fortunate, Miss Nanna, that we made our agreement when we first met, for if we had not I do not know what would have happened. You become lovelier every day, Nanna."

Yet in spite of these words Gottlieb would blush with displeasure when their meetings at the spring were disturbed by a third person.

Emilie F. Carlen

The youthful teacher and pupil continued their meetings at the little fountain, and Gottlieb at this spot gave Nanna her first instructions upon the guitar. To his great pleasure she learned quickly, and soon she was able to sing her beautiful songs to her own accompaniment on his favorite instrument.

Words are inadequate to describe Gottlieb's pride and elation when this was accomplished, and he was none the less rejoiced when he discovered how readily Nanna comprehended him when he read to her the writings of his favorite bards.

On her part Nanna replied to her kind teacher, by confiding to him all of her little plans, among the first of which she mentioned the school-room, the cat and the singing bird which he was to have, and Gottlieb gave her his advice concerning the arrangement of the benches in the school-room; the position which the black-board should occupy, and what little presents she should make her pupils as rewards of merit. He concluded by promising to send her every year a letter of advice; possibly he might come himself, occasionally, who knew?

"I am sure of that," said Nanna, one afternoon in reply to Gottlieb, as he thus expressed himself, "for when you are married you will be obliged to visit Almvik to show your rich wife to your uncle and aunt."

"Perhaps," replied Gottlieb, with a laugh, "that journey will not be necessary, for if my aunt could only have her own way, she would certainly find me a wife in this neighborhood."

"Who could you possibly marry in this neighborhood?" inquired Nanna curiously.

"Ah! Mademoiselle Nanna," replied Gottlieb, "I easily perceive that you are not in the least danger, for you can hear that your friend Gottlieb is to be married and betray not the slightest emotion."

"Why should I be moved, Mr. Gottlieb? It will have to occur

sometime," said Nanna innocently.

"And yet - "

"What yet!"

"You are a good girl."

"Ah, but don't you remember the agreement?"

"Yes, and I only intended to remark that it would not be difficult for you to adhere to it."

"Does that displease you, sir?" inquired Nanna in a tone of displeasure which was the more pertinent as it was foreign to her usual manner.

"Certainly not, Miss Nanna, on the contrary I am delighted that you should follow my advice so faithfully - either of the young ladies at the parsonage are suitable."

"Did you refer to one of those?" inquired Nanna, her countenance assuming a deathly paleness, "O they are so beautiful."

"Yes, perfectly angelic - especially Miss - Miss - what is her name?"

"You probably allude to Miss Charlotte."

"Right, Miss Charlotte, whose hair is so black and beautiful."

"O, no, that is Sophia!" exclaimed Nanna.

"Well then, Miss Sophia, I prefer her."

"But why is it that you changed their names?" inquired Nanna.

"Why, you heard that I did not confound her black hair with her sister's brown ringlets."

"How strange! Charlotte's hair is quite light!"

"Of what earthly difference is it," replied Gottlieb, "whether Charlotte's hair is brown or white, I think only of the roguish and pretty Miss Sophia."

"I think you are jesting with me, sir," said Nanna laughing so heartily that the roses instantly returned to her cheeks.

"I jest with you!"

"Of course. Miss Sophia is so serious and thoughtful that no person would call her roguish."

"Were you not as quiet as an old prayer-book the first time I saw you?" replied Gottlieb.

"And even if it was so - "

"Just look into the water, my little miss, and tell me whether you look as you used to."

"Then you would say, Mr. Gottlieb, that by some magic spell you have driven away Miss Sophia's gloominess?"

"Yes, I can say Miss Sophia's also."

"*Also?* - that is a bold speech!"

"Are you angry?"

"Oh, Gottlieb!"

"Ah, Miss Nanna. Are you weeping?"

"Mr. Gottlieb may be mischievous and tantalizing enough to compel me to do so; but this time he has not succeeded."

"Well, as I cannot force you to weep, I must confess the truth, and that is - "

"That you have seen neither of them," interrupted Nanna.

"Not that, there you are mistaken, for I called at the parsonage one evening with my aunt, and I was so much pleased with the young ladies, that now I am here with you, while they are at Almvik, where they arrived this morning. What do you think of that?"

* * * * *

What Nanna thought Gottlieb did not learn; but he soon was made acquainted with his aunt Ulrica's opinion concerning his absence. Gottlieb arrived at the latticed gate of the court-yard at Almvik, just in time to salute the young ladies from the parsonage as they drove forth from the yard on their return home. They appeared somewhat displeased, and returned Gottlieb's bow with a stiff and cold salute.

Mr. Fabian observed with pleasure, the cloud which shadowed the brow of his beloved Ulrica, foretelling the storm that was to burst forth; but not on himself.

"Nephew Gottlieb," said Aunt Ulrica drawing the young man aside, "you have to-day for the first time afforded me an unpleasant surprise."

"In what manner, dear aunt," replied Gottlieb.

"Is it your custom when in your father's house to remain away all day when young ladies are visiting your parents?"

"Nothing would have been thought about it if such had been the case. My mother is not overfond of such strict principles of etiquette."

"That is to be regretted, for boys who have not been carefully guided, rarely become gallant and well behaved young men; but we will say no more on that subject."

"In that I concur."

"We will therefore confine ourselves to that subject to which an innate knowledge guides us."

"That leads us back upon the same road."

"On the contrary, my young friend, if you will permit me to follow my own course I will place you on the road to heaven."

"Are you sure, my dear Aunt, that you have discovered the right road?"

"Certainly, only think, a ton and a half of gold; beauty, amiability, and a knowledge of cookery which excels that of Miss Nylander [The author of a celebrated Swedish cook book.] herself!"

"But love, my dear aunt, is that not to be found in heaven?"

"O, yes, and it might have already made rapid progress if you had assisted me in my first step towards the completion of my designs, by remaining at home instead of running away."

"Which proves that nothing existed before in which love could take root."

"Nonsense!" exclaimed Mrs. Ulrica, "if you wish to succeed your father you ought to improve your situation by some good marriage. Miss Charlotte is a lovely blonde, and Miss Sophia, a beautiful brunette, a perfect Spanish donna."

"Yes, she has a remarkable resemblance to a donna; but unfortunately I do not prefer Spanish ladies."

"Well, then Charlotte possesses an affectionate disposition. You cannot but admire her fine sensitive nature, which should kindle a love equalling Werther's love of Lotta."

"That is precisely what I fear. How would I look imitating Werther?"

"I do not wish you to follow his example. Charlotte is a girl for whose sake a man might act foolishly, and still be pardoned - then you prefer Charlotte?"

"No, above all things in the world I detest preferences."

"That is to say, you will cheerfully take the one of the two sisters you most admire after you have had an opportunity of visiting them a few weeks, and judging of their good qualities for yourself."

"Nothing of the kind, dear Aunt."

"Then, what do you mean?"

"That I have a great desire to look out for myself in this matter; and that taking all things into consideration, I am much too young to think of marriage."

"Then you despise your aunt's assistance?"

"God forbid that such a sentiment should ever enter my heart. I honor and love God. I am grateful to Him that He has given me a heart, and I pray Him not to send me a bride which that heart cannot love."

"Your words sound well; but I shall not have my little plot marred by them. Will you or will you not, accompany me to the parsonage, and conduct yourself as you should before the young ladies?"

"I will behave politely towards any young lady; but, aunt, if you have any other meaning concealed beneath those words then - I will say no!"

"You wish to quarrel with me, then. Do you understand what

that means, my dear nephew?"

"I dare not think of such a misfortune."

"Yet that misfortune will certainly come. God knows I would do much for you; but consider upon your words while you have yet time - you need not trouble yourself to be present at the fishing excursion this evening."

"Why so, aunt, am I outlawed?"

Mrs. Ulrica Eugenia assumed an air of haughtiness.

"Then I have fallen into disgrace," continued Gottlieb.

"I will not deny," replied Mistress Ulrica, coldly, "that you are on the road to disgrace; but I hope this wholesome lesson will cause you to think better of my exertions in your behalf."

"Of that I have my doubts," thought Gottlieb as his aunt majestically left the room; "and yet perhaps it is foolish on my part not to take her advice. - Oh, why is not my little nymph of the fountain the possessor of a ton and a half of gold? - The little creature - hm - She is really too beautiful!"

CHAPTER XI

THE FISHERMAN

The usually turbulent lake Wenner, presented, on the evening of which we are about to write, an unruffled and mirror-like appearance. In its clear bosom was reflected the lofty cliffs of mount Kinnekulle, and sloop after sloop passed over this gigantic image until a puffing steamboat dashed over it and the picture was lost in the foaming spray in her wake.

Almvik was situated on a truly romantic spot near the margin of the lake, of which a magnificent view could be obtained from the mansion. The surface of the lake this evening presented a pleasing spectacle. Fishes were leaping out of the water near little boats which were swinging at anchor, or were being pulled by sturdy fishermen who were going forth to ensnare the subjects of the water Queen; but the proud Queen, who, from her crystal palace beheld the danger, commanded her subjects to retreat, and quickly the sportive fishes hastened to the depths of the water that afforded them a barrier through which their enemies could not break.

In consequence of these manoeuvers on the part of the water Queen, our friend Mr. Fabian, who frequently endeavored to capture her subjects, was invariably unsuccessful. Undoubtedly this must have been a source of much misery to the poor man, for he was situated between two iron wills, namely that of his wife and that of the water Queen; the latter would not pay tribute, while the former demanded with all the firmness of an absolute monarch, that the tribute should be forced from the water Queen at all hazards.

After the above explanation our readers can well imagine Mr. Fabian's feelings when after having congratulated himself that his wife's anger with her nephew would occupy her mind for the entire evening, he received a summons from her that the boat and fishing tackle were ready for use.

Fishing was one of Mistress Ulrica's favorite pastimes, and although she did not generally participate in it, yet when she observed her husband's unskillfulness, she would indignantly cast aside her parasol, and grasp the fishing rod. However it may be, whether the water queen below wished to compliment the earthly queen above, - we know that ladies are prone to be polite to each other - or that some truant fish remained behind to become an easy prey to the enemy, suffice it to say that Mistress Ulrica was generally fortunate; but she did not - as she might have done - make use of her advantage, as she herself would say, "to cause her husband to blush with shame."

When the dutiful husband arrived at the landing, he found his tender wife, standing near the boat, clasping her child's hand in her own, and our friend was obliged to see that his jewels were safely seated in the boat. After he had rowed the skiff out as far as Ulrica thought was proper, he with many misgivings threw out his line.

"How strange it is my dear Fabian, that every time you fish you sit still there on your seat like a perfect automaton!"

With this preamble, Mistress Ulrica opened the floodgates of her ill-humor, to which on occasions like the present especially she gave perfect freedom.

"An automaton, my dear!"

"A post, a perfect post. You do not even turn your head; just as though the company of your wife and child was the most wearisome thing of your life."

But dearest Ulrique Eugenie, I must keep watch for a bite. If I turn around - "

"You would not lose the sense of feeling if you should; but you hope, I suppose, that persons on the shore will think you master of the boat. Simpleton! What folly to think that!"

"Dear Ulrique Eugenie, shall I ask if you have spared my nephew your ill-humor that you may vent it on me. It is my opinion - "

"What is your opinion, sir?"

"O nothing further than that I am sufficiently burdened with your natural bad-temper already, without having it increased by the aid of another."

"Burdened! - ill-humor - bad temper! - is the man mad? Do you thus speak to me, your wedded wife, who bears your stupid indifference; your want of tenderness and love with angelic forbearance? O, this is too much! It is shameful! It is undeserved!"

"Now, now, Ulgenie, do not be so hasty. You know how patient I am."

"And what am I, then, to be married to such a musty husband? Your wife is courted before your very eyes; you see nothing! you hear nothing! - I could be unfaithful to you, and even then you would close your eyes. O, fate! O bitter life! such a husband can drive a wife to desperation, and from thence it is but one step to madness."

"Who is again playing the gallant to you?"

And in this "again," reposed an expression which displayed that such scenes were not new to him. Mistress Ulrica, like

Emilie F. Carlen

other women, possessed her weak points, one of which was that if a gentleman happened to converse with her pleasantly, she immediately imagined that he was desperately in love with her. But to her great sorrow, Mrs. Ulrica, although she possessed entire control over her husband's actions, never could make an Othello of him. Had Mr. Fabian but known her desire in this respect, he could have deprived his wife of her sceptre, and taken up the reins of matrimonial government himself.

A tyrannical husband would have been able to bend Mrs. Ulrica like a reed, and to have trodden her under his feet which she would willingly have kissed; but now Mr. Fabian kissed her feet, and therefore she crushed him to the dust, and although she did not merit the reproach that Desdemona received, it was, nevertheless, no fault of his. But of what use would it have been even should she have merited it? Othello was a fanciful creation which her husband of all men would have been least willing to personate.

"My Fabian," she would say to herself, "my Fabian can never prove unfaithful to me. He is too much of an idler, and thinks only of his sofa, pipe and tobacco."

But we will resume the thread of the worthy couple's conversation.

"Who is again making love to you?" inquired Mr. Fabian again.

Mrs. Ulrica uplifted her reproachful eyes to Heaven. "He asks who! he has not even observed it!"

"No, my dear wife, I have not."

"And yet he has this entire day - ," she turned her face aside, feigning to conceal a blush.

"To-day! Why we have had no gentlemen guests to-day, except

the pastor's assistant who came with the young ladies, and took his departure before they did."

"No gentlemen guests! As if he, the accomplished scholar, and entertaining gentleman, was nobody! and it was nothing that - "

"Well, what further?"

"That he, carried away by those charms, that you have so long observed with indifference, should become deeply smitten with me."

"What! Do you think he entertains a secret affection for you?"

"Affection, I will not say affection; but passion, which word your dull brain cannot comprehend, you virtuous and modest Joseph!" the lady laughed at her own joke, and then continued, "I am not certain whether I had better tell the young man that I have discovered his hope; but I shall be forced to forbid his visiting me, which will be the same as telling the whole world how this delicate affair stands."

"Will you permit me to give you a little advice?" said Mr. Fabian.

"Why not, Fabian, you are my husband, and as such you have the right to do so."

"Then I would say, drop the subject where it stands."

"Are you not fearful! Do you not shudder at the possibility of an unpleasant event?"

"O, my dearest Ulgenie, can I for a moment doubt your strength of soul, your virtue?"

"It is true I am thus strongly armed, and I thank you, my dear Fabian, for confiding in my faithfulness." - As was usual a few cheering sun-beams followed the cooling shower. - "Forgive me, my dear husband, for harrowing your feelings; but there are times when even the strongest minded are weak."

"You are an exception, my love."

These confident words had nearly renewed the vexation within Mistress Ulrica's bosom; but suddenly she was struck with an idea that caused her to assume a still more affectionate expression of countenance.

"We will trouble ourselves no more concerning that deeply to be pitied young man. I have something else which I wish to confide to you."

"Another lover?" inquired Mr. Fabian, widening his eyes.

"I refer to a youth, for whose welfare I am deeply concerned."

"Explain yourself, my dear."

"Fabian, you must not hate him, for the young man does not understand himself, this I will answer for with my life, and perhaps he only indulges a platonic affection for one who realizes the romantic ideas which his youthful imagination had formerly brought forth."

"You do not mean Gottlieb, do you?" inquired Fabian, unsuccessfully endeavoring to conceal a laugh.

"Fabian, why do you speak so sardonically? If in spite of your watchfulness, his has, unobserved by you, paid a tribute to your wife's beauty, you must remember that he did not know he was sinning. It was merely an accident that made me acquainted with the secret of his heart."

"Will you permit me to inquire what that accident was?"

"With pleasure. I had - I tell you this in confidence - I had chosen one of the pastor's daughters as his wife; I invited her to Almvik to-day, but he avoided her presence. He retired to that solitude which he seeks every evening either before or after we go out on our drive. A certain instinctive sentiment causes him to leave the house when you are absent, and more than all, when I reproached him for his faults, and pointed to the advantageous match I had in view for him, he had the boldness to say that he would retain to himself the right of disposing of his own heart."

"And do you believe, my dear, that you are the first cause of this trouble?"

"I have felt grieved at the thought that it might be so, nothing further."

"Well, well, dear Ulgenie, I will release you from this burden on your conscience."

Mr. Fabian, who always found it a difficult matter to converse long upon a serious matter, spoke the above words in a tone of voice especially lively, for his heart was rejoiced at the thought that now he had an opportunity of ridding himself of an unwelcome guest, without giving cause for any one to believe that it was his own desire to do so.

"What are you babbling about?" inquired Mistress Ulrica, sharply, "what do you know about my nephew's affairs?"

"Nothing further than that he has had a little love affair of his own, which occupies his attention during those solitary walks you referred to a moment ago."

"He! Gottlieb! Has he dared to fall in love!"

"Certainly."

"Impossible!"

Emilie F. Carlen

"But I assure you that it is true, and if you will ask him why he so frequently visits the valley, he certainly will not deny that he goes there for the purpose of meeting handsome Nanna, the daughter of old Mr. Lonner. He reads poetry to her, and under the pretence of teaching her the guitar, he finds an opportunity of pressing her pretty little white hands."

"If that is true. If he, while he remains under my roof, enters into such a miserable intrigue, I will - for I consider it my duty as occupying the place of his mother - I will to-morrow morning mar his plans. But how did you learn this?"

This was a question which Mr. Fabian could not truthfully answer, for if he should do so, he would have been obliged to state that he, after his disagreeable parting with Magde, had taken a roundabout path towards Almvik, which conducted him so near the valley that he discovered two persons sitting beneath the tree near the fountain, and that from that day forward he had closely watched Gottlieb's movements, so that he might be enabled to hold a weapon over the one who might perhaps be a spy upon his own actions.

It was therefore an accident which opened Mr. Fabian's eyes to Gottlieb's crime; but he had not wished to play the part of an accuser, O, no, for such love affairs were common to all young men, at least he thus assured his wife.

"Make no excuse for him, sir," interrupted Mistress Ulrica sharply, "this indeed is excellent, and will become still richer if not prevented in time. The reproaches of a mother on the one hand, and the curses of a father on the other; a seduced girl, perhaps something worse; a criminal investigation, and a scandal in which our house, and possibly ourselves, will figure largely; all this we must expect. As true as my name is Ulrique Eugenie, this matter shall have an end, and a speedy end, too."

"But how will you accomplish that?" inquired Fabian.

"That I shall attend to myself. Gottlieb has said that he should like to travel over the mountains into Norway. Now then he can go to Amal, and from thence he may commence his journey. He shall have money, but must obey me."

* * * * *

The following morning, after Mistress Ulrica had convinced herself by her own eyes of the truth of her husband's report, for she followed Gottlieb to the meadow that morning instead of taking her usual ride, Gottlieb was summoned to her apartment, and underwent an examination that nearly exhausted his entire stock of patience. The interview resulted in his determination to accept his aunt's proposal, that he should take a journey into Norway. He did not inform Nanna, however, of the cause of his sudden departure, for he feared that it would grieve her.

Their last interview was cheered by bright anticipations of the day when Gottlieb should return and observe the improvement which Nanna should make, both in her performance on the guitar, and in her education; for when his aunt had made a contract of peace with him, Gottlieb had insisted that Nanna should have the guitar, to which clause the old lady consented.

The young couple parted in the hope of a joyful meeting, and Gottlieb's farewell kiss did not assist Nanna to forget him.

The next day after Gottlieb had taken his departure, Jon Jonson's sloop arrived in the bay opposite the little cottage in the valley.

CHAPTER XII

GRIEF

Nearly two months had elapsed since those remarkable days on which Nanna had received her first kiss, and Magde had heard from her husband by the arrival of Jon Jonson's sloop.

Great had been her joy when Ragnar's gifts arrived in safety. - She then thought that everything had come to a good conclusion. But greatly was she deceived! There was a man to whom Magde had invariably conducted herself with cool indifference, and who, after having been defeated by her in the manner which we have before described bestowed upon her a parting glance which had caused her to shudder as if she had trodden upon a serpent. And he was indeed a serpent in human guise, for soon she felt the delayed sting of the venomous reptile.

Until Ragnar had received his appointment as mate, old Mr. Lonner had invariably purchased his supplies of the merchants at Goteborg; but as Ragnar thought that foreign goods could be obtained much cheaper by procuring them himself, and sending them home without paying the duty, he soon persuaded the old man to adopt his opinion on the subject.

Until now no unpleasant consequence had resulted from Ragnar's occasionally smuggling a few articles for the use of the family; but the old adage says "a pitcher which goes oft to the fountain is soon broken," and in Ragnar's case this proverb was verified.

Yet, for this accident, the custom house officers were not so much to blame, for not one in that service would have thought for a moment of searching the cottage in the valley, unless positive information was received, nay more, unless that information was accompanied with threats of exposure, for dereliction of duty. Unfortunately, the custom house stamp was wanting upon the handkerchiefs, shawls, and other goods sent by Ragnar, and the family not only were deprived of them, but were menaced with fines and penalties, which to pay, was entirely out of their power. To add to their misfortune their protector, Ragnar, who would have soon put an end to their troubles, had started a few days before the catastrophe, upon a voyage to Brazil.

Magde and Nanna wept only when they were alone, or at least when they were with each other. They concealed their tears from the old man, his life should not be further embittered; it was bitter enough already. The little fortune on which they had hoped to subsist for many months was entirely swept away. Old Mr. Lonner, however, observed the secret grief of his daughters, and said to himself:

"Poor children, you do not know what is yet to come."

The smuggled goods were marked with old Mr. Lonner's name only, and he well knew that a heavy penalty was yet to follow.

"We have enjoyed so much happiness, and peace, since Ragnar and Magde were married," said he encouragingly to his daughter, "that we should bravely endure a little misfortune. It is not allotted to man that he should enjoy a constant season of prosperity."

But Nanna and Magde smiled sorrowfully as he thus spoke. The inmates of the cottage now exerted themselves to the utmost to better their sad condition. Our friend Carl exerted

96   Emilie F. Carlen

himself beyond all the others. He who had neglected the affairs of his own relations for those of his neighbors, now scarcely had leisure to step beyond the boundary line of his father's estate. He was everything, and did everything so willingly and skilfully, that it was not necessary for the family to hire any servant to assist them as they had formerly done, and although latterly he had been somewhat feeble in health, he cared not for himself, but worked manfully in wet as well as dry weather. His troubles and toil were all forgotten, when Magde would reward him for his efforts with a friendly nod of her head.

And when she would say, "You will work yourself to death, my Carl," he would laugh pleasantly, and immediately renew his efforts ten fold. He now determined that after his duties at home were performed, to go among the neighbors; not to be a nurse for their children, as before, but to work for wages, and after this when he returned and placed the money on Magde's weaving loom, a bright object might have been discovered glistening upon the crumpled bank-note. It was a tear of joy which Carl had shed.

Magde after the first occurrence of this incident, dared to praise Carl no further. She already perceived the consequence of so doing, but after the lilacs and lilies had faded, the tulips, roses and lavender bushes, bloomed, and however weary Magde might find herself after a day of toil, she would each evening place elegant boquets in Carl's flower vases.

At length, and too soon, the decision in regard to the smuggled goods arrived, and as Mr. Lonner was unable to pay the penalty imposed upon him, he was doomed to imprisonment. In this their day of trouble, Mr. Lonner alone retained his courage.

He well knew in truth to whom they were indebted for their distress, but he feared nothing. He trusted in the belief that Magde would do all that was in her power to raise the sum of money necessary to pay the fine. It was unfortunate, however, that Magde, without the old man's knowledge, had expended their small stock of money to pay a few debts that they had contracted the previous spring.

We will not attempt to depict the misery of the moment when old Mr. Lonner stepped into the boat which was to conduct him to the prison at Harad which was located on the opposite side of the lake, and where he was to be confined for the time being. Both of his daughters wished to accompany him to the opposite shore; but he forbade them so seriously that they dared not press their desires further.

It was touching to observe these sorrow stricken females, amidst their terror search high and low in the cottage for various articles of comfort for their beloved father. At length, with a slight degree of sorrowful impatience old Mr. Lonner ordered the boatmen to push off from the shore, and then it was piteous in the extreme to behold both Magde and Nanna, as they clung to the gunwale, to whisper their tearful adieu's, and to promise that they would pay him a visit in his prison in a few days.

Finally the bitter moment was over; the boat rapidly proceeded from the land; but so long as they could discern the old man's white locks fluttering in the breeze and even until the boat appeared a speck in the distance, Nanna and Magde remained on the shore gazing out upon the water.

In the meantime Carl without the knowledge of the family had proceeded to the opposite shore of the lake, and when the boat which contained his father touched the shore, Carl greeted him tenderly and presented him with a ten dollar bank note. This was a treasure indeed, and Carl had obtained it by selling the only article of value which he possessed. It was a silver watch, which his mother had given him before she died.

On his return home that evening he remarked: - "Father need not fear. He can live in his prison rolling in riches; a gentleman met him on the other shore and loaned him ten dollars."

How Magde and Nanna blessed the kind hearted gentleman; but their joy was but momentary. What should they do now? How should they provide for themselves in this unexpected trouble. Their poor neighbors like themselves, were moneyless, and their wealthy neighbors would undoubtedly require some security before they would loan them money.

Nanna often looked towards the spot in the meadow, so full of pleasant memories. If her kind friend would only return. He certainly, would be able to advise them how to act in their present strait.

Three days elapsed after the old man's departure, and many were the plans formed by Magde, but the only apparently feasible one, was that which she would most unwillingly undertake to carry into effect. She was perfectly convinced that the proprietor of Almvik would willingly assist her; but he would do it *too* willingly, for afterwards he would cause her to feel that she was in his debt.

"But," thought she in a maze of doubt and fear, "what shall I do? Is it better to remain as we are and allow the poor old man to languish in prison, or to go to Almvik, and thus receive the only boon our father wishes, liberty? But what would Ragnar advise me to do. He loves his father as he does the apple of his eye; but his wife he loves as he does his own heart - And then if he should imagine that Mr. Fabian H --- Oh! my God! what trouble would then arise! - but again I shall not be able to assist the old man - no, no, that will not do, I can hold out no longer."

Magde had no person with whom to consult, for what advice could poor Carl give? Nanna was a mere child, and Magde felt that she could not consult her upon such an intricate question.

She had conversed with the parson concerning her trouble, yet although he was not backward in giving her good advice, he nevertheless refused to assist her with his purse, for he was as miserly as he was wealthy.

The time had now arrived when Magde could no longer postpone the promised visit to her father, and all the members of the family wished to go upon this little pilgrimage. Great were the preparations that were made to supply themselves with a sufficient quantity of provisions which they were to take to the old man. Magde baked pan-cakes, and Nanna made pies, and if a smile did appear on Magde's lips it was when they spoke of the pleasant surprise they were preparing for their father.

At length the moment for their departure arrived. Even little Christine and the favorite dog Carlo, were to form a portion of the company, that they might be able to see their old friend. The children leaped with joy.

They thought only of the pleasant trip over the swelling billows of the lake. Magde finished lading the skiff; but her heart was overflowing with grief, for she had no glad tidings with which to gladden the heart of the old man.

Nanna who during the busy activity of the morning had successfully endeavored to suppress her sorrow, was so much overcome as she was about stepping into the boat that she nearly fainted. She saw in her imagination the pale and suffering countenance of her father; who was however smiling patiently as he stood ready to greet his children, that were to leave him again in his dreary and lonely prison.

The poor child in anticipation suffered all the pangs of a second farewell with her imprisoned parent.

"It will not do for you to accompany us," said Magde in a firm and motherly tone, "you are ill, and therefore had better return."

"I am afraid," replied Nanna trembling violently, "that I shall be obliged to do so. Give my love to him, and tell him - " and now her long suppressed tears burst forth in torrents - "tell him if I do not come, it is not because I do not love him."

"Silence, silence my poor sister, I know myself what I have to say - Go and may God be with you - here is the key - Lock the door - Carl take the oars."

CHAPTER XIII

THE BANISHMENT - THE RE-UNION

When Magde's boat passed the mansion at Almvik, two persons were walking on the verge of the shore near the lake. The one was Mistress Ulrica, and her companion was Gottlieb, who had returned a few days before, from his trip through Norway.

As the boat shot round a rocky point of land, Gottlieb exclaimed, as he recognized its occupants, and bowed friendly to them: "Where are they all going! They look so sorrowful and dejected!"

"Sorrowful!" repeated Mrs. Ulrica, "you may thank God that it is not necessary for you to participate in the sorrows of the lower classes."

"If they are in trouble, I do not see why I should not sympathise with them."

Aunt Ulrica shook her head with a dissatisfied expression of countenance.

"You may certainly boast of your firmness of mind, and your knowledge of human nature; I have shown you the danger of associating with such persons. I sent you away - I - "

"I beg your pardon," interrupted Gottlieb, hastily, "I was not *sent* away. I took a journey which I had decided on myself, and returned as I departed, with a heart ever ready to sympathise with the afflicted."

"Then go, and participate in the sorrows of your beggar friends. I suppose, from your liberal words, that you are well supplied with money."

"What has happened to them?"

"The old man, in connection with his son, has been detected in smuggling foreign goods, and of course his property was confiscated. The old gentleman in whose name the business was transacted, was sent to prison because he had no money to pay the penalty, and there he will remain until you go to his release."

"And he shall not wait long," replied Gottlieb. "I have accomplished greater undertakings than that in my time."

"Ah, ha," sneered Mrs. Ulrica, "you speak boldly, boy. I am astonished."

"If any one should be astonished, I am the person."

"Indeed!"

"I come to relatives who at first welcomed me cordially. My affections attached themselves to my kind friends, for it is a necessary quality for me to be grateful; but suddenly everything is changed, and I am treated like a school boy, whom you must curb, or else fear that he might commit some folly. To this description of guardianship I have not been accustomed, and as it is not my desire to submit to your control, I must beg you, Aunt Ulrica, not to attempt to govern me in this manner, for I assure you that your efforts will always be fruitless."

"Foolish boy! You forget that I could be useful to you; could smooth your path by my wealth and influence."

"I do not forget it, and I should have been very happy to have been able to retain your good will; but at the price of my liberty of thought and action, I do not desire your favor."

"Then you will return to the valley, to Miss Nanna."

"Undoubtedly. She requires my presence, and I long to see her."

"Then you still love the young girl?" inquired Mrs. Ulrica.

"I do not know whether I loved her when I departed from Almvik; but this much I do know, that her image has been with me constantly during my absence; and that I shall see her again to-day."

"To tell her of this folly?"

"O, no, that would be unjust, as I can tell her nothing more."

"Thank Heaven for that! You, yourself, see that it would be impossible to - "

"What?" inquired Gottlieb, as his aunt paused.

"To marry her."

"I do not at all consider it impossible; but as it is uncertain whether I ought to wed Nanna when the time arrives for me to marry, it is better for both of us that we should rest satisfied with friendship alone."

"Listen to me, Gottlieb. Sometimes you speak so wisely that I am not certain but that it would repay me to make a proposal to you."

"Well, I am all attention."

"If I am not much mistaken, pity is the only sentiment that you feel for that girl, Nanna. If I was to take it upon myself to pay the old man's fine; if I should further promise you to provide for Nanna's future maintenance - you know I would not break my word - will you bind yourself not to see her again?"

"No, I will never do that. She would be oppressed with sorrow throughout her whole life, if I should be capable of making such an unworthy promise."

"Obstinate youth! you force me to perform my duty to your mother my sister, and command you to visit Almvik no longer. I will not burden my conscience by abetting you in your misconduct."

"I will remain a few days longer," replied Gottlieb without evincing the slightest emotion, "to rest myself after my journey, and then I shall be ready to obey your command."

"Right," muttered Mrs. Ulrica hotly, as she hastily left the young man, "you shall repent this."

Without wasting time by thinking upon this conversation with his aunt, Gottlieb hastened on the road towards the little cottage. He had observed Nanna was not in the boat, and after proceeding to the spring, and fruitlessly searching for her, he hurried to the cottage, his heart beating with such rapidity as he stood before the door, that he was astonished at his great emotion.

"Illness could not have prevented her from going with them," thought he, "certainly not, or they would have remained with her."

Thus thinking he knocked at the door; but he was obliged to repeat the summons several times before he heard the sound of slow footsteps approaching.

"Who is there?" inquired a soft voice from within.

"'Tis I, Nanna!"

An exclamation of joyful surprise was the only reply. The bolt was quickly thrown back; the door opened, and Nanna appeared upon the threshold, pale and careworn. She was clothed in her only holiday dress, a black merino frock which fitted closely around her neck, thereby disclosing her graceful bust to its best advantage.

Without speaking, but overwhelmed with her joyful emotions, she cast herself in Gottlieb's arms, and never was there a purer embrace given or returned than on this occasion. With tender gentleness Gottlieb imprinted his second kiss upon her lips, and then said softly: -

"Poor Nanna, poor child, you have at least one friend in your adversity."

"Then Gottlieb is acquainted with - " She blushingly withdrew herself from his embrace. She had not thought that her greeting had been contrary to customary usage.

"Yes, I know your sorrow; and you may rest assured that I will give myself no rest, during the few days that I remain here, until I see your father at liberty and safely in his own house again."

"O, if that were but possible!" she clasped her hands and lifted her eyes, confidingly, to the face of her youthful friend.

"It shall be possible, Nanna. You have my word for it. If I had been here it would not have happened."

"I thought so. An inner voice told me that if *he* would only come to us all would be well again."

"I am grateful for your confidence and shall always remember it with pleasure."

"Remember it!" exclaimed Nanna, "are you going to leave us again?"

Nanna again clasped her hands, and this action and the mournful expression of her countenance spoke more than words could have expressed.

"Will you miss me, Nanna?"

"Always."

"And perhaps wish we had never met?" inquired Gottlieb earnestly.

"Ah, no," replied Nanna warmly, "the remembrance of you will perhaps work a happier future for me than I would have had without it."

"But tell me," said Gottlieb changing the subject to one less dangerous, "why did not your sister apply to the proprietor of Almvik."

"O, she would never apply to him. She would rather allow things to take their own course."

"Why so?"

"I know not whether I dare tell you. Papa and Magde, consider me a mere child, yet I can understand that Mr. H -- has sought her with wrong motives, and if I can believe my brother, Carl - "

"What then?" interrupted Gottlieb eagerly.

"Then I can believe that all of our troubles have originated in the fact that Magde refused to give that gentleman a kiss when he requested it."

"What, did he wish to purchase a kiss?"

"Yes, for Carl's pardon," and now Nanna related every circumstance connected with the theft of the game, in nearly the same words in which she had heard it from Carl.

After a short season of reflection, during which he compared the different circumstances, Gottlieb arrived at the same conclusion that Carl had expressed to his sister; and at the same time he also fancied that he had discovered a method for old Mr. Lonner's release, which could not fail of success. In the meantime he merely inquired whether Mr. Fabian H -- had visited the cottage since his discomfiture.

"I have several times observed him prowling about the premises," replied Nanna; "he probably hoped to have an opportunity of seeing Magde alone, which however he has never had, for even should he offer his assistance, she would not have dared to accept it, for if she did, Ragnar would be very angry."

When Gottlieb returned to Almvik, he learned that his worthy uncle, whom as he before knew had left the house early that morning, was not expected to return until late in the evening. In consequence of this unfortunate circumstance, Gottlieb saw nothing before him except a vexatious delay in his intended operations; but it soon entered his mind that Mr. Fabian's absence might be connected in some degree with his wayward love. The day on which he had visited Magde, in order to take advantage of Carl's theft, he had also departed from Almvik in the morning, for during the evening hours his wife was invariably on the watch.

The more Gottlieb considered this circumstance the more he was convinced that if his uncle had sown the seed it was done for his own benefit, and undoubtedly the time was now at hand when he should reap the harvest.

"Ah!" thought Gottlieb, "if I should only be so fortunate as to obtain a power over my uncle, my suspicions and conjectures would exert a powerful influence upon his yielding disposition, especially, if I should place his wife in the back-ground. But to surprise him, with my own eyes in forbidden grounds, would be as good as to have old Mr. Lonner safe back in his cottage again."

CHAPTER XIV

THE PRISONER

While the incidents last narrated were transpiring on the one side of the lake, Magde's boat had reached the other, and the occupants of the boat were about landing, yes, Carl had even secured the boat to the stake, when one of the little ones in attempting to reach the landing, fell overboard with a loud cry.

The young and always self-possessed mother, answered the boy's cry, not by crying out herself, but by springing into the water after him, and when Carl turned to learn the cause of the confusion, she had already reached her little boy, and was holding him up at arm's length out of the water. It was all done in a moment, without the least unnecessary confusion.

"Carl," said she quietly, "take the boy."

But Carl had lost his self-possession entirely. After he had literally thrown the boy on the landing, he inquired with a trembling voice: -

"Could you not wait for me? The boy would not have sunk immediately."

"You must not scold me, Carl, I am only a little wet."

She then quietly drew herself to the shore.

"How will you dry yourself now?" inquired Carl in a tone of uneasiness and vexation.

"O, easily, I will call on Mother Larsson and borrow a dress to wear while we visit our father, and my clothing will be dry by the time we return."

Carl was silent. He was displeased because Magde had not called him to her assistance. Meanwhile he proceeded with the children to the prison, that he might prepare the old man for the visit. Magde did not tarry long at Mother Larsson's. As soon as she had obtained the necessary garments, she hurried on, clothed in a neat peasant's frock which fitted her fine form gracefully.

The prison at Harad was located in the ruins of an old castle. Its outward appearance presented a dark and forbidding aspect. The heart of the beholder would contract within him as he gazed upon those ruins of fallen greatness, as they reposed before him, dark and deserted, like an evil omen in his path.

But the interior of the prison, with its tottering weather beaten projections, apparently ready to fall from their resting places, presented an appearance still more gloomy and forbidding. Dampness, and mould of a hundred years growth had obliterated all traces of the fresco paintings that had formerly ornamented the ceiling, on which the moisture had gathered and fell at regular intervals with a hollow patter upon the stone pavement below.

The places once occupied by glittering chandeliers were now shrouded with immense spider webs, in which a whole colony of spiders lived subsisting on the noisome vapors of this gloomy charnel like abode.

Aside from these poisonous insects, an occasional rat, and a few unfortunate prisoners, there were no other inhabitants in this dark prison. A flock of jackdaws had built their nest beneath the eaves of the old castle, and as they received good treatment from the prisoners they would pay them a passing visit at their grated windows to look in upon them or to receive a few crumbs of bread. Old Mr. Lonner had already made their acquaintance and derived much pleasure from attending to their little wants, while he anxiously awaited the arrival of his children.

When Magde arrived she found Carl had prepared the way for her so that she, without hindrance, proceeded directly to the old man's cell. Mr. Lonner was deeply moved by the visit of his children; but he appeared perfectly resigned. Magde's two children were seated upon his knees, while Carl was standing before him relating all that had transpired during his imprisonment. The cloud which had rested upon the old man's brow changed instantly to an expression of joy when he beheld Magde the wife of his beloved son, enter the room. His arms trembled as he embraced her, and his heart throbbed painfully when she described her sorrows and troubles, and told him that Nanna had nearly fainted as they were about entering the boat, at the mere thought of the second parting.

"It was right to leave her behind," said Mr. Lonner, "and if we can only find some means whereby I may be released before the autumn, that the cold may not increase my feebleness, then - "

"Means must be found, father, I think, of immediately going to the city, to take our cow and the two sheep with me, aside from those I will also take the piece of linen which I have made for Ragnar's shirts. By adding all these together I - "

"But, dear daughter, if you sell the cow, how will these little ones prosper?" He clasped his hands upon the two little white heads of the children who were sitting in his lap.

"O, I can borrow some milk of our neighbors, and we can repay them in the fall, after Ragnar returns, for then we shall have another cow."

"That will never do, my child. We must discover some other method."

"I had an idea, also," said Carl, advancing from a corner into which he had withdrawn when Magde entered.

"What is it, my good boy?" inquired his father.

"I was thinking about that which Ragnar has so often told us, about the people in England who procured money by pawning themselves - what was it he called it?" continued he, scratching his head to arouse his memory.

"Life Insurance, was it not?" replied his father.

"That's it, father, and Ragnar also told me that even here in Sweden, gold might be obtained from England on such terms. Now, if we could find some one who understood this matter, and would undertake to draw up the proper writings, I would willingly give my life as security, and then you see, father, I should be just the same as so much ready money."

"My good son, your words are well intended; but it is not as you think in relation to Life Insurance."

"O, that is too bad, father, or you might have received a large sum of money when I am dead."

"My life, I hope, will be finished before yours," said his father, "I am old, and you are young."

"True, I am young in years; but lately, yes, last Friday, while I passed through the church yard, I heard a voice, and that voice I believed."

"What ideas you invent!" exclaimed Magde, frightened for the first time, as she observed Carl's hollow cheeks and sunken eye, "but what did the voice say?"

"'Carl, Carl, Carl,' it said, calling my name three times, 'you will not live long.'"

"Your brain is weak, my boy, because you have worked too hard. When your body has received rest, and rest it must have, you will feel much better. But tell me, Carl, what you thought when you imagined you heard the voice."

"I did not think, but merely replied, 'indeed.'"

"But, Carl, with this superstition you will make your father sorrowful."

"Sorrowful? I do not think so. Should he be sorrowful because our Saviour in his grace is willing to call me to his fold? Instead of being sorrowful, the day of my departure should be a festive day. How many troubles do we escape after we are placed in the earth!"

"But if you think in that manner, you will become mournful yourself, you will not be able to laugh any more."

"Not laugh," replied Carl, and without an effort he commenced laughing merrily. His face glowed with mirthfulness, and his melancholy humor seemed to have vanished as if by magic. It appeared so strange to him that Magde should desire him to laugh, that he forgot all about the life insurance or the warning voice, and once thus engaged, he took no farther part in the consultation.

An hour elapsed, and Magde, after having emptied the basket of its contents, experienced a return from the hope that had sustained her during the interview, to her former despondency, as the moment of parting approached. Carl proceeded in advance to prepare the boat.

"In four days, at the furtherest, I shall return," said Magde, pausing upon the threshold of her father's cell, "and then, as I hope for Ragnar's continued love, I shall bring you good tidings."

"Thank you, my dear Magde. Ragnar shall learn all that you have done for his old father. Kiss Nanna, poor little innocent, for me, and tell her that she must not come here, for it will only make her heart more heavy and sad."

A moment later, and the creaking doors resounded throughout the ruins, the prisoner was again alone.

But once more did he hear a dear voice, for when Magde arrived at the outside, she remembered with a feeling of uneasiness, that her youngest child had not been blessed by its grandfather. In the haste of departure, the little one had been entirely forgotten; but as it was impossible for her to leave the prison with the dear child unblessed, she stood beneath the grated window, and exclaimed:

"Father, dear father, please look through the window, and I will hold up the baby for you, that you may give it your blessing."

Immediately the old man's white head appeared at the window, and Magde held the child aloft in her hands towards him.

And now everything was performed rightly; the last farewell glances were exchanged, and then Magde and her children disappeared from the old man's sight.

CHAPTER XV

GOTTLIEB ON THE WATCH

The heat of the day had been followed by the pleasant coolness of an August evening. The hands of the clock pointed to the hour of ten, and Gottlieb, who had been walking during the entire evening in the neighborhood of the little red cottage, began to think that his uncle Fabian had in all comfort reached his home by another road.

"It is so quiet in the cottage," thought he, "that I think they have all retired."

He glanced stealthily over the lilac hedge towards Magde's window. The entire valley was bathed in moonlight, and the moonbeams glanced directly through the window panes of Magde's apartment, with such vivid brightness that Gottlieb was undecided how to act.

Soon, however, he resolved to convince himself of the true state of affairs, that he might be prepared if his uncle should arrive.

He gradually made an opening in the hedge and having found his way clear before him he advanced to the window which, as the weather was warm, was secured only by a small cord. He glanced through the window, and a beautiful picture met his gaze. In this chamber, the husband and wife's little temple, the moonlight was brilliantly reflected from Ragnar's brightly polished hunting and fishing implements which, neatly arranged, were hung against the walls.

At the opposite side of the room, a much worn sailor's hat, commonly called a tarpaulin, was balanced upon the point of a fishing rod, and beneath this trophy was placed a small side board, the open doors of which disclosed a number of shelves laden with gilt edged drinking vessels of white and blue china; a set of rose colored tea-cups, and several polished silver plated mugs. A few uncommonly excellent specimens of carving in wood, decorated one of the shelves, and another shelf contained several articles of jewelry which Magde had received both before and after she was married. All these little valuables Magde had gathered together, after she had put the children to bed, in the hope that she might find some few articles among them that would save her from disposing of the cow.

But her search, undoubtedly, had proved fruitless, for Magde's ornaments were made almost entirely of bronze.

Seated in a chair with her hand resting upon the cradle, Magde was now sleeping soundly.

She had been called, probably, while she was engaged in assorting her little treasures, to attend to the wants of her infant, and overcome by fatigue had unwillingly submitted to the power of that consoler of human grief, sleep. Her face was turned towards the window, and the moonlight illumined her entire figure, which was rendered more prominent by the fact that the cradle stood in the centre of the room. She was still attired in the garments she had borrowed, and her brown hair, fell in two long braids over her loose white sleeves, from whence they dropped upon the face of the sleeping child, while Magde's elbow was resting upon the little pillow.

"What a picture for a painter!" thought Gottlieb. "Young Lonner is not the most miserable of men, by my faith; but I know one who at some future time will look much prettier in that position!"

The dull sound of a horse's hoofs, aroused him from his reveries.

"Ah, ha," thought he as a smile of triumph played upon his lips, "I was right. We shall now see what is to happen."

Gottlieb returned to his hiding place in the hedge with noiseless rapidity. He had not remained long in his somewhat tiresome position, when the sound of the horse's hoofs ceased, and from the noise which proceeded from the other side of the hedge he concluded that the owner of the horse had dismounted and was securing his animal to a tree.

He soon heard the sound of light footsteps proceeding over the grass, and then he discovered the familiar form of Mr. Fabian approaching the cottage. After the new comer had assured himself that the door was fastened he advanced to the window near which Gottlieb had been standing a moment before. Instead of spending time in useless watchfulness he immediately tapped upon the window; but Magde slept so soundly that the noise did not disturb her.

Mr. Fabian flatted his nose against the window pane and suddenly discovered the picture that Gottlieb had so much admired. Yet it was not an expression of love which passed his lips as he gazed upon her.

"Confound that woman!" he exclaimed, "she drives me mad, and I believe she would look on, if I was parching with thirst in the torments of hell, and not give me a single drop of water."

He again tapped upon the pane so loudly, that a person less fatigued than Magde would have awakened. At this moment Mr. Fabian was struck with fear at his own temerity.

"Only think," thought he, "suppose I should awaken some one else! What if an account of this should come to my wife's ear!" - the thought was terrible, and the guilty husband's knees trembled violently. So much did he respect his "dear Ulgenie," that he felt it even at his present distance from her, and perhaps he would have relinquished all his plans in relation to his beautiful Magde, had he not discovered that the window was fastened only with a small cord.

To break off a small twig from a neighboring bush, and to thrust it through the crevice of the window and remove the cord from the hook, was the work of an instant, and before Gottlieb could fully understand the nature of his uncle's movements he saw him suddenly disappear through the window.

Of course Magde was now awakened by the noise of Mr. Fabian's abrupt entrance, and she quickly sprang from the chair. When she recognized the intruder she was seized with a deathly fear; which was however but of momentary continuance. With flashing eyes, and haughtily curling lips she advanced towards him with a bearing so threatening that Mr. H -- retreated in fear.

"Why do you visit me at this hour?" she inquired.

"I was unable to come earlier. I have been to see the justice and made such arrangements that I think Mr. Lonner can be released as early as to-morrow."

"And to speak these words - undoubtedly well intended - you have crawled through my window."

"Upon my honor it was not my fault. I knocked several times, and not wishing to go home without telling you this good news, which I thought would cause you to sleep better - and observing you had not retired - I seized the only opportunity remaining."

"Well," replied she, "I do not think harm will result from your friendly visit, but as it is out of the order of things that you should remain here, I must request you to leave the room in the manner you entered, and then I can converse with you through the window."

"Cruel Magde!" exclaimed Mr. Fabian entreatingly, and even dared to extend his hand towards her. But Magde repulsed him with a look of scorn and anger.

"Travel no further upon this crooked path, and call me Magde no longer, I bear the name of my husband, and wish to be called by that title alone."

Gottlieb who could observe and overhear all that occurred, or was said in Magde's chamber, could scarcely refrain from laughter as he saw his good uncle retreating before the virtuous woman until he arrived at the window from which he somewhat clumsily descended. Gottlieb was on the point of rushing forward to receive his loved relative in his arms and thus preventing him from injuring his precious limbs, when the sound of Magde's voice prevented him from rendering this important service to his uncle.

"There, that will do," said she, "we can now converse without inconvenience to either of us. I hope Mr. H -- has not hurt himself."

"O, never mind me," replied he, "your heart is too hard to be moved at my sufferings."

"I wish to say a word to you, Mr. H --. Your labor is entirely thrown away upon me. I can pity the folly of a man if his folly is not evil; but - "

"Am I evil? Try me," interrupted Mr. Fabian hastily.

"I will," replied Magde. "If you will bind yourself to release my father I shall ever be grateful for the service."

"And nothing further?"

"Nothing."

"Then, at least give me your hand that I may with it wipe away the tears that scald my eyes. I am a weak, a tender hearted man, and must weep when I am scoffed at. But never mind, give me your hand, a moment."

"It is impossible."

"Give me but your little finger."

In lieu of a reply, Magde endeavored to close the window; but her admirer prevented her from doing so.

"Ah!" exclaimed he furious at his defeat. "You wish to enjoy a boon, and not reward the donor. Then listen, the old man shall remain where he is. If I do not interest myself for him no one else will."

"That remains to be seen. Mr. Gottlieb has returned - "

"Ah! then, he has returned. Well, what can he do?"

"Not much, my dear uncle," exclaimed Gottlieb advancing towards Mr. Fabian, "except to give my dear aunt Ulrica, a full account of the interesting conversation I have accidentally overheard."

"Without replying Mr. Fabian stared a moment in bewildered surprise, at the intruder, and then rushing wildly to his horse, he mounted and urged the animal to a furious speed.

"Well, well," exclaimed Magde, "we can well compare Mr. H - - to a hare. But Mr. Gottlieb, whatever chance brought you here, do not bring sorrow upon him, by speaking to his wife of this adventure."

"Fear not, Mrs. Lonner, I have not been on the watch here to become an informer; but as I heard certain things from Nanna to-day, and as I from the first have suspected my uncle, and as I wished to have him in my power - "

"I understand you Mr. Gottlieb. You are an honest and faithful friend, and we shall never forget - "

"And I, Mrs. Lonner," interrupted Gottlieb, "I shall not forget this valley I assure you, and now good night; in a short time everything will be as it was before."

"Thank you, a thousand times! When Ragnar returns, through God's assistance we will repay you."

* * * * *

Gottlieb's heart bounded with joy, as he proceeded on his road towards Almvik, but the heart of another traveller in the same direction was oppressed with gloomy forebodings. It is almost unnecessary to say that the latter traveller was Mr. Fabian H -- . On his arrival at Almvik he entered his wife's chamber trembling with anxiety, lest Gottlieb had been there before him.

"What is the matter with you?" inquired his wife, who had already retired to her bed; "has the horse been balky, or have you met with an accident?"

"Nothing, nothing, darling Ulgenie; but my head has been heavy all the afternoon."

"That is caused by your excessive sleeping," said Mrs. Ulrica.

"Perhaps it is. Hereafter I shall sleep less, and after this, my dear wife, I will follow your advice in everything."

"Then, my dear, you will be a good husband. If I should always find you so, I would not have so many causes for complaint."

Emilie F. Carlen

"Have you any complaint to make now?" inquired Mr. Fabian, anxiously.

Mr. Fabian was in a state of fearful suspense. The air to him appeared populated with evil spirits.

"I did not speak thus for the purpose of troubling you, dear Fabian, it would not be just for me to choose this moment, when you feel so repentant, to remind you of other moments when you do not seem impressed with the worth of your wife."

"Yes, yes, that would indeed be cruel, for it is true, really true, that - that - "

"What, Fabian, good Fabian?"

"That I never before have so much esteemed and adored you, my dear, dear - " He was unable to proceed.

"Ah! Fabian, that is the true spirit. You at last understand how happy you are."

"Yes, as happy as the condemned sinner," sighed Fabian; but in such a manner that his wife heard the first word only.

CHAPTER XVI

THE FESTIVAL

The next morning, when Gottlieb awoke, he discovered that he had a visitor even at that early hour of the day. His uncle Fabian was pacing backward and forward at the side of his nephew's bed, with a countenance so wretched and woe begone, that Gottlieb could not but pity him.

"Good morning, uncle," said Gottlieb, cheerfully, "how is your health?"

"Why do you ask?"

"Your voice sounds just as if I was a robber demanding your purse or your life. What is the matter?"

"That which you told me yesterday makes your comparison very apt."

"You are mistaken. It is not my intention to play the part of the famous Rinaldo Rinaldini. I am the most peaceable person in the world, and if you wish to remain at peace at home - which is very natural, you know - I have no desire to prevent you from doing so."

"But, perhaps, you intend to demand from me three times the sum of money necessary to fee a lawyer, to bribe you to secrecy."

Emilie F. Carlen

"Shame upon you. I have not demanded anything. I only expect - "

"What?" inquired his uncle.

"That you will of your own free will and accord loan me the money necessary to pay old Mr. Lonner's fine. In a few months, when Ragnar Lonner returns and repays me, I will settle with you. If he does not repay me, why it is but a small sum to lose."

"And what will you require for yourself?" inquired Mr. Fabian.

"Shall I peddle out my secret like a Jew? I swear by my honor that I will not divulge to my aunt one word of all that has passed."

Mr. Fabian thrust his hand into his capacious pocket, and withdrawing his purse, with a sigh counted the money into Gottlieb's hand.

"I shall not give you my note for this, for if I am not repaid I do not expect to repay you."

His uncle did not immediately reply, but after opening and closing his purse several times, he addressed his nephew in a tone which displayed deep and true emotion.

"Gottlieb," said he, "I am not miserly. You have spared me when you might have prepared a place of torment for me. I am grateful. Have you any debts? Your father is not rich."

"That is spoken like a man of honor and a true relation," said Gottlieb, warmly, "but fortunately I have always been obliged to live economically, and therefore have escaped from falling into the foolish habit of contracting debts."

"Well, then, if you have no debts, you at least have a future to prepare for. You must not therefore refuse my offer."

"I do not wish to make use of it at present. Yet I do not wish you to consider it refused entirely. At this moment I do not require anything, unless indeed you wish to spare my feet and my boots, by giving me a little money to pay my travelling expenses. When the time comes, and I find myself fully engaged in my father's office, I will consider your proposal with the greatest pleasure."

"Do so, and I will have a good memory, I assure you."

"One word more, uncle. You must promise me to trouble the worthy Mrs. Lonner no longer. She will never submit to your desires."

As he thus spoke, an ashy paleness o'erspread Mr. Fabian's countenance, and with a shudder he glanced fearfully around the room.

"O, the walls have no ears," said Gottlieb; "but uncle you will promise me this, will you not."

"Most assuredly," replied his uncle. "That woman has driven me almost mad; but I think that last night's fright has entirely cured me. I shall not go there again under any circumstances."

* * * * *

The songs of the birds of the valley were more melodious than ever before, the perfume of the roses and lilacs were sweeter than formerly, at least so thought the occupants of the little cottage when Gottlieb visited them that afternoon. Certainly, however, the feast which was given on that day had never been equalled before, except perhaps on the day of the arrival of Ragnar after a long absence from his wife and home.

It was a splendid dinner - roasted spare ribs, and fish, and cakes. The old man occupied the seat at the head of the table. Gottlieb, who had provided this repast from the money he had received from his uncle for travelling expenses, was seated

Emilie F. Carlen

beside Nanna. The children ate so rapidly and heartily that it appeared as though they intended to swallow a sufficient supply to last them for a year to come. Carl, wearing his Sunday vest, a vest that Magde had made, and with a rose in his jacket button-hole, a rose that Magde had plucked, was seated in his usual place at the table, cheerful and contented. Magde attended almost solely to the old man's wants, filling his plate, and replenishing his cup. And lastly, little Christine, who trotted from place to place, taking care of the cow, dog, sheep, goats, and the ancient cat, was as happy and cheerful as the others. Altogether the scene was beautiful and harmonious.

"And for all this happiness," said the old man, looking tearfully upon the youth, "for all this happiness, Mr. Gottlieb, next to God, we are indebted to you. Happy must be the parents of such a son!"

"Father Lonner," said Gottlieb glancing around the table, with a friendly smile, "you have no reason to be envious."

"That is true," replied the old man nodding his head pleasantly to the circle of beloved ones.

In the afternoon, after the old man had retired to his comfortable bed, now doubly comfortable to him, to rest himself awhile, and Magde was seated by his bedside pleasantly chatting with him, while Carl was busy making little boats for the children, Nanna and Gottlieb were seated near the spring beneath the tree, in the meadow.

It could easily be believed that the young couple were not very talkative, for Nanna was busily engaged in searching in the grass for a four leaved clover, and Gottlieb was amusing himself, according to his childish custom, by blowing shrill blasts upon a thick blade of grass.

It was sunset. The glowing reflection of the sun fell upon Nanna's pale neck and face, illumining them with a golden blush.

"I am sorry," said Gottlieb, at length, throwing aside the blade of grass, and assuming a serious cast of countenance, "I am sorry that our lessons must have an end; but all is for the best, for, my child, you know enough already."

"More than enough," replied Nanna, softly.

"Especially for a school teacher," said Gottlieb.

"Yes, especially for a school teacher," repeated Nanna.

"But you speak so abstractedly. You are not so lively as usual."

"I did not know it; but if Gottlieb says so, it must be true. When one has been so glad as I have been to-day, and then as sorrowful, it takes much courage to meet the change indifferently."

"But, dear Nanna, you were aware that I should be forced to go away soon."

"I did not know that you were going so soon as to-morrow morning."

"Neither did I, myself, when I saw you yesterday; but when I determined to go by the steamboat, you perceive that - "

"Yes, yes."

"And then again what difference will a day or two more or less make, when we part - "

"Never again to meet," interrupted Nanna.

"You will do right in the meantime not to hope too much."

Nanna glanced inquiringly towards Gottlieb.

"Do you not think it strange, Nanna, that we who have been

Emilie F. Carlen

acquainted but so short a season, should think so much of each other?"

"It is perfectly natural that we should. Persons in fashionable society cannot become so well acquainted with each other as we could in one hour. At first we met each other every evening, then every morning and evening, and at length - "

"And at length morning, noon and night!" interrupted Gottlieb, with a smile. "In truth, Nanna, you are right, for if our every meeting was so divided that we should be together but once each week, our acquaintance would have been prolonged for an entire year."

"O, much longer than that even," said Nanna, joining in Gottlieb's laugh.

"And as we have remained by our agreement not to fall in love with each other, we part as friends, and not in despair, and what is still better, not with reproaches, which, had the case been different, we would have been obliged to make and listen to."

"Yes, it is fortunate, very fortunate, that - that - " stammered Nanna, unable to finish the sentence.

"We need not conceal from ourselves that in making that arrangement we ran a great risk. For my part, I am not too proud to say that it has been very difficult for me to keep it."

"But Gottlieb," replied Nanna, "as you have kept it, it is better as it is."

"Certainly; but then it is not so good as I wish to have it."

"How do you wish it to be then?" inquired Nanna innocently.

"Upon my honor I can hardly say; but if I was placed in better circumstances - " Nanna dropped her eyelids over their soft tell-tale orbits; but not so quickly but that Gottlieb detected a ray of hope gleaming from their deep wells.

"Will you advise me what course to take, when I have obtained a competency?" continued Gottlieb.

"No, that would be of no use; but Mr. Gottlieb, when I hear that you have wedded the rich wife of whom you have spoken, I will rejoice at your good fortune."

"And does not the thought of that rich wife cost you even half a sigh?"

"Not if that wife will render you happy."

"Nanna, you speak as though you did not love me at all!" exclaimed Gottlieb hastily, forgetting entirely the part he had determined to play during this interview.

"And should I love you?" inquired Nanna blushing deeply. "I think I am not such a foolish girl as that."

"But I believe that you love me," replied Gottlieb. "Can you deny that your heart is mine?"

"I do not deny it; but I shall not allow it to be so," said Nanna with a glance that immediately cooled Gottlieb's sudden ardor. "My heart is my own, and should not be an object of trouble to you; and I assure you Mr. Gottlieb that I shall not allow any weakness on my part to cause you to break the judicious contract we have made."

"Ah! Nanna, you are both wise and charitable. I shall not endeavor to wrest the secret from you; but you are so much esteemed by me, that at some future day, when I can follow my own inclinations I will return to you."

"I will forget these last words, Mr. Gottlieb, for I think them the saddest you have ever uttered."

"You are right; but I spoke as I thought. It is not my fault if I thought that you were above all others most suitable to become my wife."

As he thus spoke Nanna trembled violently and she looked upon him with a gaze which contained more bitterness than words could have expressed.

"I believe I am mad indeed. I have endeavored to speak in a better spirit, and instead of so doing - I had better go immediately - or - "

"Or what?"

"Or I will, yes, I will, hold you to my heart, and swear to you, as true as I am an honest man, that I love you, and you alone, come what may, I can withhold myself no longer." Gottlieb suited the action to the word, and enfolded the blushing girl in his warm embrace.

"O, Gottlieb!" cried Nanna, weeping and laughing, "this is madness indeed!"

"No, on the contrary it is happiness!"

"But to-morrow you will repent it!"

"Never, Nanna, I sincerely believe that all is for the best. We can work hard; we have only a few needs, and it is such happiness to love each other."

"But - "

"You must accustom yourself to omit that disagreeable word. When my mind is once made up, I permit of no *ifs* nor *buts*. And as we do not require a great amount of money to defray our little domestic expenses, I think it would be wrong for us to waste the best part of our lives in useless delay. After one year has elapsed, the parson shall unite us as man and wife, and

I shall take you from this valley, and we will look forward to all the joys and sorrows, which our Heavenly Father in his wisdom shall send us."

Nanna, who for a long season had battled against the intoxicating desire which had filled her heart, gradually assented to Gottlieb's words, and the interview terminated with a second agreement, which was directly contrary to the first one, for by it they bound themselves to love each other forever.

They agreed that this change from their former agreement should be concealed from all others. They alone should know the secret.

CHAPTER XVII

RAGNAR

Autumn arrived.

The valley was strewn with yellow leaves. The birds had ceased their songs. The grass had withered. Rains and storms had discolored the fountain. Yet, although Nature seemed to have been engaged in contentious strife, still joy reigned supreme within the little cottage. Ragnar, the beloved husband, the darling son, had returned. Seated in the midst of his children beside his lovely wife, and with his arm encircling her waist, he listened with a countenance changing from cheerfulness to solemnity to a recital of all that had transpired during his absence.

As soon as Mr. Lonner, for he was the narrator, had concluded, Ragnar advanced and enfolded the old man in his arms.

"What viper did this? I have a strong suspicion - to cast such an old man into prison - and I was away from you, unable to protect you and these weak and deserted women."

As he thus spoke, his countenance glowed with indignation.

A slight cough at the other side of the room attracted Ragnar's attention. It was Carl.

"I understand you, Carl," said he, "you must pardon me. I forgot myself when I said the women were deserted."

And the frank and honest Ragnar, whose ruddy brown countenance bespoke his health, advanced and extended his hand to Carl, who with a face as sickly and yellow as the seared leaves without, was reclining upon the sofa, watching the family group with a restless eye.

Poor Carl, each day he gradually faded, and his belief in the warning voice he had heard in the church yard became firm and unwavering. He accepted Ragnar's proffered hand with a grateful smile.

"How hot you are!" exclaimed Ragnar, "I will hasten to the village and speak to the physician."

As Ragnar thus spoke, Carl laughed in his peculiar manner. "That will be profitable indeed!" said he.

"Certainly it will, dear Carl," said Magde, approaching the sick youth, "Ragnar is right."

"Ragnar is always right," said Carl, in an unusually sharp tone, "so long as you please him you do not care if you neglect my wishes."

"What, Carl, do you not love your brother?" said Ragnar, in a tone of reproach, at the same time pressing a kiss unobserved, as he thought, upon his wife's lips. Ragnar always felt an inclination to conceal from the observation of others the fact that he still loved his wife as he had when he first wedded her, and therefore rarely caressed her when in the presence of witnesses; but on this occasion, his affection was so great that he could not resist the pleasure of stealing a kiss.

"Is not the entire room large enough for you to kiss in without my seeing you?" said Carl, harshly, "I do not wish you to do so right before me."

"Perhaps you envy me," said Ragnar, with a laugh. He had not given Carl's expression a serious thought.

Carl lifted himself upon his elbow, and gazing full in his brother's eyes, he replied slowly and firmly, "Yes."

"Why do you, Carl?" inquired Ragnar.

"Because I do not wish any body to kiss Magde - is it not so, Magde? You well know how I behaved myself when Mr. Fabian H -- wanted to buy a kiss of you."

"What! I believe the poor boy is mad! What! Buy a kiss of Magde! Poor Carl!"

"Am I speaking false, Magde? Answer me."

"O, Carl, how strangely you tell your story!" exclaimed Magde, "you ought first to have related how it happened, and - "

Magde flushed and paled alternately, and in her excitement could scarcely express herself.

"Can there be any truth in this?" said Ragnar, and his eyes sparkled.

Magde had now recovered her presence of mind, and related, without concealing a single fact, all that had happened between herself and Mr. Fabian.

"I am now firmly convinced that this - this - no matter, that Mr. H -- was the prime cause of our father's imprisonment."

"He was," interrupted old Mr. Lonner. "I am as firmly convinced of it, as I am that the young man of whom I have spoken was the cause of my release. I wish you were acquainted with Mr. Gottlieb. He is a worthy young man."

"I will tell him so in the letter I shall write him; but what if he entertained the same desire that influenced Mr. H --".

"Fear not for me, at least," replied Magde, casting a roguish look towards Nanna.

"Ah! that is singular indeed; but after all Nanna will bear a pretty close inspection - but I cannot drive that Mr. Fabian from my mind."

"First you must tell us some of your adventures," and Magde's countenance wore such an entreating expression that her husband understood her immediately; and therefore as long as he remained in the presence of his father, and his sister and brother, he continued speaking of all the singular things he had seen and heard, which was listened to by a pleased and expectant audience.

At length the time arrived when the husband and wife were at liberty to interchange their thoughts freely; the children had been nicely tucked in their little beds, and Ragnar and Magde alone occupied their private apartment.

"Now, dear Magde, now you must give me a good kiss. God bless you for this happy moment. After tossing six months upon the ocean, it is a joy indeed to return to one's own home and wife."

"Is it true indeed, dear Ragnar, that you love me now as you did when we were married?"

"Did you find no four-leaved clover last summer, that you ask me this question?"

Without replying, Magde hastily opened a clothes press, and produced an old compass box, from which she took a handful of withered clover leaves.

"See here," said she.

Emilie F. Carlen

"And do these not convince you?" inquired Ragnar.

In this old box, Magde preserved, so to speak, the tokens of her wedded joys. From the first year of her marriage, she, whenever her husband was absent, would seek in the meadow for four-leaved clovers, under the conviction that so long as she continued to find them, she might rely upon the continued love and fidelity of her husband. And she was invariably successful, and each year she deposited the clover leaves in the old compass box. As Ragnar uttered his last question, Magde cast herself upon his breast, and gazed tenderly into his face.

"O don't look at me too closely, to-morrow I will look better, after I am washed and dressed," said Ragnar, arranging his shirt bosom, and smoothing down his jacket collar.

"You are so good already, that if you should be better it would be dangerous; but Ragnar, you have forgotten to measure the children to see how much they have grown since your departure. You used to do that as soon as you entered the house after a return from a long voyage."

"This time," replied Ragnar, "you greeted me with such strange news that I quite forgot all my usual habits. It grieves me to observe that Carl is upon the verge of the grave. True, he was ill last winter; but he soon recovered."

"He exerted himself too much during our troubles," said Magde, "then he has taken no care of himself, and then - yes, yes, there is something very strange about Carl."

"What do you mean by strange, Magde?" inquired her husband. "Do you think that he is really insane?"

"Oh no, I did not mean that; but - "

"Speak on, speak your mind."

"Now, do not laugh at my fancy - or be vexed with poor Carl.

I think that - he loves me too much, and his passion has weighed heavily upon him, although he does not, himself, understand it."

"Your words are worthy of reflection, Magde; now I remember, his conduct did appear peculiar when he said he envied me the privilege of kissing you. Poor fellow, how could I be vexed with him? He, probably, never desired to vex either you or myself."

"Never. Frequently during the summer I have placed flowers in his room, and in them he took his greatest delight. Even now he loves to hear me sing to him, or to read a chapter in the Bible, above all other things."

"Such love," said Ragnar, "is a beautiful rose, the perfume of which cheers a drooping spirit. He may continue his love; it will sustain him in his last trial. Hereafter, I will not even take your hand in his presence."

"How kind you are, dear Ragnar. Now I can be to him as I was before your return." Magde wiped the tears from her long eyelashes, and before Ragnar could question her, she continued: "You may depend upon my fidelity. I only wish to afford him a slight ray of joy while he is still on earth. Without me he stands alone."

"Act your own pleasure, my dear Magde, you are aware that I confide in you as in my own heart. Although I shall act gently towards Carl, who with his own desire, would not injure me, still I will not be so submissive with an individual like Mr. H --, who has conducted himself most wrongfully."

From these words Magde became aware that she would be obliged to relate all that had occurred between Mr. Fabian and herself, and this she did accordingly.

She feared more from Ragnar's silence than she would if he had given vent to his rage in words. Ragnar possessed a faculty

Emilie F. Carlen

of controlling his anger by a silence which was much more impressive than furious speech.

"Ah, then he entered your window, after he had first removed the old man. Well, well, worse things have been done before."

This was all he said; and as not only the following, but also the second day passed, without Mr. Fabian's name being mentioned, Magde thought that Ragnar had looked at the affair with sensible eyes. She even felt somewhat annoyed at the thought that Mr. Fabian's punishment should be so light.

CHAPTER XVIII

AN HOUR IN MISTRESS ULRICA'S CHAMBER

Throughout the entire fall, Mr. Fabian had been his "sweet Ulgenie's" humblest slave, and therefore had been trod deeper into the dust. Since he had learned of the return of Ragnar Lonner, he had suffered a feverish anxiety. Even his easy chair no longer afforded him rest, for sleeping or waking, one object alone was constantly before his eyes: Ragnar Lonner's wrathful countenance peering through the door.

He was suddenly seized with as strong a desire for active life, as he formerly possessed for easy rest, and he felt himself in no safety except when at a distance from the mansion, for he knew that Ragnar possessed too much honor to entrap him in an ambuscade.

One morning, when he, as had been his custom for the previous week, went to his wife with the information that he was compelled to take a short journey, she sharply accosted him:

"Man, what does all this restlessness mean? Are you insane? Am I always to be left at home alone?"

"Ah, my dear," replied Mr. Fabian, "you are aware that I must attend to my business."

"I know that not long since you found it difficult to take care of yourself. This sudden change in your disposition will never do."

"Dear Ulgenie, I acknowledge your superior judgment; but to-day I really must attend the auction at Rorby, there is to be a sale of some genuine Spanish sheep."

"Ah! as that is really some business, you may go; but come home early."

"I hope to return before eleven o'clock."

Mrs. Ulrica presented him her hand to kiss, and after he had pressed it to his lips with all the gallantry which was still left him, he quickly turned away from her.

Mrs. Ulrica during the entire day was filled with wonder at the sudden change that had taken place in her husband, and if she could have for a moment entertained such a thought, she would have believed that her husband had become acquainted with some intriguing female.

But among her female acquaintances in the neighborhood, there was not one whom Fabian had not seen at least twenty times, and he had undergone each new ordeal with a firmness which proved that he was out of all danger.

This point once settled, Mistress Ulrica was more composed, and after having spent the day in attending to her domestic duties, she retired to her bed at an early hour, for she always felt weary and ill-humored when her Fabian, whom she really loved, was not at home to hear her tender words and reproaches.

About an hour had elapsed after Mrs. Ulrica had fallen asleep. The servant also slept soundly, for, although she had been told to wait for her master, she had satisfied her conscience by leaving the hall door unlocked - contrary to her mistress' strict command - and then retired to her bed.

As before said, Mrs. Ulrica had been asleep about an hour, when she was disturbed by a singular noise which resembled the shuffling of feet near the bed. She opened one eye that she might warn her husband that one of his first duties should be not to disturb his wife's slumbers. But the warning produced no effect. This being the case, Mistress Ulrica found it necessary to open the other eye, that by the aid of the night light she might discover Fabian's true condition.

She first glanced towards the sofa; it was empty. Then she looked towards the easy chair; but as this stood partially in the shadow of the large bed curtains, she was able only to perceive a pair of feet, and it was these very feet that had the impertinence to shuffle in her room, without asking her permission.

"Fabian," she exclaimed, "are you not ashamed of yourself? What are you doing?"

But Fabian did not reply.

"Ah, you foolish man, I see now that you have been made drunk, you could not withstand their entreaties, poor man; please prepare for bed."

And yet no answer.

"He is as drunk as possible. Go to your own room, Fabian; be careful, do not take a light with you, and do not fall down stairs and hurt yourself. Are you going to move to-night? Shall I ring the bell for the servants, that they may carry you to bed?"

Not receiving a reply, Mrs. Ulrica tore aside the bed curtains, and extending her hand, placed it upon a strange head of hair.

"Heavens!" she exclaimed, "that is not my husband!"

Emilie F. Carlen

"What of that, it is the husband of another," replied a calm voice.

Terror prevented Mrs. Ulrica from crying aloud. "A thief!" she gasped.

"I do not think so," replied the voice.

"Who are you then?" stammered she.

"Sleep quietly, you shall not be disturbed."

Mistress Ulrica continued to feel for the bell cord. "I believe," said she, "he wishes to murder me when I am asleep."

"Sleep quietly, I neither wish to steal nor to murder. I only wish to - "

The unfortunate cramp, which at her first terror had attacked Mrs. Ulrica's throat, now suddenly disappeared, and she emitted a long and loud scream; but no sooner had this been accomplished, than a large brawny hand was placed roughly over her mouth.

"Please do that no more," said the voice, "or I shall be forced to be troublesome, and do not look for the bell-rope, it would only be disagreeable for you if the servants should enter the room now."

"What do you want then, fearful man?"

"To remain where I am. At present I want nothing further."

Suddenly a new light dawned in Mrs. Ulrica's brain. What if he should be an unfortunate suitor for her love.

"How?" said she, forcing all her pride and dignity into her words, "how? remain here? Sir, this is my bed-room."

"I am aware of the fact."

"And here no man has a right to enter except my husband."

"And myself," added the voice.

At this unexpected reply, the lady summoned courage to examine the unabashed visitor more closely. He was an elegantly formed man, and as he gazed at her with his expressive eyes, interest and repugnance were both created within her heart. The repugnance was caused by the fact that the man wore a blue frieze coat, which unfortunate garment at once dispelled her romantic dreams.

"Will you explain the cause of this unheard of impertinence?"

"That cause will very soon arrive."

"Very soon? You did not seek me then?"

"Not precisely."

"Then probably you wish to see my husband?"

"Yes."

"Am I at all concerned, then?"

"Slightly."

"Ah!" exclaimed Mrs. Ulrica, who now remembered her strange visitor's first observation, "there must be a mystery about this which I do not understand. You remarked that you were the husband of another."

"True."

"And furthermore you said you had a right to seek my husband in this room?"

"You certainly know your alphabet."

"Then you have - O, what will become of us! - you have - a demand to make of my husband."

"No, he has a claim on me, and this I will pay back, principal and interest."

"O, the monster! The crocodile! He has been untrue to me."

"Yes, both in heart and desire; but my wife is not one who cries out, or attempts to pull the bell-rope. She commands respect without so much trouble."

"And do I not, also?"

"I do not know what you would do, if you should see a man, at this time of night, crawl through your window, and attempt to bring you to disgrace by the promise that he would release an old father from prison; but I do know you have nothing to fear at present."

"You are then Mr. Ragnar Lonner?"

"I am."

"And for such a miserable reward - that woman - "

"What! Miserable reward! - that woman! - Well, that night lamp is not very brilliant, but I can easily perceive that I have before me an old dutch galleon, so badly rigged and managed, that I would prefer to crowd sail and make my escape rather than to take her in tow. And you call my wife that woman! Miserable reward!"

"I do not understand your gibberish, my good man: but that you are unrefined and uneducated I can easily see, and I command you to quit my room immediately."

"You would then force me to retreat, as my Magde drove back your husband. Please try the experiment."

"Monster! Unfeeling wretch!" exclaimed she, "is this the manner to speak to a lady, to an injured wife who is obliged to bemoan the infidelity of her husband. O, the villain! I will overpower him with my wrath!"

"My turn comes first," interrupted Ragnar.

"Ah, ha, I understand. My cup is filled to the brim - blood must flow - Lonner do you wish to kill my husband, then?"

"To fight with him. God forbid. Such things I leave to people of rank. I have another method of doing my business."

"And what is that?"

"O, it is very simple. I thought that nothing would be more unpleasant to him than to be placed in a disgraceful position before his wife, and perhaps a greater punishment for such a miserable man could not be devised than to - but no matter, your husband knows why he leaves his house every day."

Mrs. Ulrica clapped her hands together violently. Now the riddle was solved. She now knew the cause of the sudden change in her husband's conduct.

"And, as it has been impossible to find him at home in the daytime," continued Ragnar, "I have come this evening to settle with him in this place, and at this hour."

Ragnar had scarcely ceased speaking, when heavy and slow footsteps were heard ascending the stairs.

Like an infuriated tigress waiting for her prey, Mrs. Ulrica, enveloped in her crimson shawl, sat up in her bed; her eyes flashing with rage, and her face flushed to a redness which outvied the crimson of her shawl. She was awaiting the approach of her husband.

Ragnar arose, and as silent and unmoved as a statue awaited the entrance of Mr. Fabian. Ragnar had not produced a dagger or sword; but he drew forth from under his loose jacket a cowhide of the greatest elasticity, and the best quality.

Without dreaming of the terrible storm that had gathered, and was about to pour down upon his devoted head, Mr. Fabian entered the apartment. But the moment his eyes fell upon the forms of his wife, the doom pronouncer, and Lonner the genius of revenge, he staggered back towards the door, and had not his legs refused their office he would have sought safety in flight; but at two stern glances, one from Lonner, the other from his wife, he sank powerless to the floor.

And yet, if ever, this was the time for him to assume the character of Brutus. And what better cause had he to arouse himself from his stupor, than that Lucretia had received a male visitor in her bed-chamber. True, Mrs. Ulrica had not received an insult, neither did she appear prepared sacrifice herself, like Lucretia, as an atonement for the outrage. All in all, present appearances were well calculated to arouse sterner sentiments within Mr. Fabian's heart; but he was so frightened that he would have forgiven everything if he could have assured himself that the horrible spectacle was but a dream which would vanish at the coming of the morning.

"Perjured traitor!" screamed Mrs. Ulrica, "you hide yourself like Adam after his fall. But come forth, this Lucifer will teach you that you no longer dwell in paradise."

"Mr. Lonner," stammered Mr. Fabian, "I am an innocent, unhappy man, and I swear to you that Mrs. Magde has never - "

As he heard these words Ragnar trembled violently.

"Silence, reprobate," said he, "the name of my virtuous wife shall not pass your lips. She needs none of your recommendations; but *your* wife, you pitiful coward, she shall learn from me, now, what your true character is."

Thus saying Lonner with one hand seized the unlucky Fabian by the coat-collar, and brandished the horse-whip over his head with the other.

But as Mr. Fabian made no resistance, but wept and begged for mercy in loud and wailing tones, Ragnar released him, and, confused at the singularity of his own sentiments, he glanced towards Mrs. Ulrica, and said:

"He is so cowardly, that it seems almost as bad to whip him, as it would be to beat a hare. In giving him over to you I am fully revenged."

The cow-hide disappeared beneath his coat, and Lonner departed.

But Ragnar Lonner had made a miscalculation, when he thought that Mr. Fabian would fall into the hands of the Medusa within the bed-curtains. The very thought of the humiliation he had undergone, and the fear of what was yet in store for him, inspired Mr. Fabian with an unusual degree of courage or rather drove him to desperation.

Brutus aroused himself. He could see no other method of escape than by crushing the tigress before she pounced upon him. He therefore at once attacked her with passionate actions and wild expressions.

"O, you miserable woman! You faithless wife! Do you think that I shall allow myself to be blinded by the farce you have just played with your lover? I will leave you alone in your house. I cast you from my heart. The whole world shall know you as I know you now."

"Fabian! Fabian! are you mad?"

Mistress Ulrica was both frightened and pleased. This was a scene she had long desired.

"If I am mad, who has driven me to madness?" shouted Mr. Fabian, determined to retain the advantage he had already won. Then assuming an imposing position he gazed sternly into the face of his trembling wife. "How long I have closed my eyes to your little indiscretions! How many bitter tears I have shed, when I observed how you encouraged that shark who made love to my wife while he feasted at my table."

Mistress Ulrica, who was suddenly changed from a tigress into a lamb, assured her husband that she was innocent; that she had not even entertained a guilty thought. But as she humbled herself, Mr. Fabian's wrath increased, and astonished that he had not long before discovered this method of taming his wife, he played the tyrant *con amore*. He accused his wife of so many things, that she, humiliated and crushed, fell on her knees before him, and entreated him to restrain his rage until he had ample proofs of her guilt. This boon Mr. Fabian H -- finally condescendingly granted, and like an indulgent pascha, entreated by his favorite slave, he at length permitted her to slumber at his side.

This entire change of government was effected in the short space of one hour.

The sun was high in the heavens when Mistress Ulrica awoke. At first she could not distinctly remember the drama which had been performed the preceding night; but when all the events were brought clear to her mind, she sighed deeply. Her destiny was entirely changed; but after a few moments' reflection, she determined to submit to her fate, and become the one who should obey, not command.

While she was meditating in what manner she should refute the charges brought against her by her husband, she was interrupted by a truly soft and persuasive voice, which said: -

"Sweet Ulgenie, dearest wife, can your heart be touched? I dreamed last night that I might dare approach it."

"Oh, so you have noticed me," said Mrs. Ulrica, immediately assuming her former authority, when she found herself thus entreated. "Have you slept out your debauch?"

"Was I - is it possible that I was inebriated? I have quite forgotten what happened last night."

"You fool, when were you able to remember anything unless *I* reminded you?"

The perusal of a continuance of this scene will scarcely repay our readers. Suffice it to say that Mr. Fabian's reign of one hour remained thereafter a legend only. Like all other unsuccessful revolutions, it was followed by a government still more exacting and severe.

CHAPTER XIX

CARL

Winter had departed. Ragnar, the bold seaman, had left his home, and his ship was ploughing the broad ocean. The grass in the valley waved gracefully in the light winds of spring. The children once more launched their miniature boats, and the occupants of the cottage all labored for the good of the little commonwealth.

But there was one of the family who could not mingle in their labors, and who sat quietly in his corner, gazing cheerfully upon the operations of the others. It was Carl.

During the winter Carl had been confined to his bed, but at the present time he occupied his father's arm-chair, which the old man had relinquished to him. He usually sat in a corner near Magde's spinning wheel and his father's bed-room door.

When the children returned from their out of doors sports, they would sit on the floor near Carl's chair, and listen to the many tales of fairies, nymphs, and sea gods, that he told them in a pleasant but weak voice, while he as formerly made willow whistles and repaired their little boats.

The neighbors' children also visited the cottage that they might hear his last stories, and they all brought with them many little gifts that their mothers had prepared for poor Carl. At a later period the mothers came themselves, bringing their own presents, which they carried in large baskets, for there was not one in the entire neighborhood for whom Carl had not performed a service, and without a solitary exception they all loved him.

Then who was to take his place, after he should be taken from his friends. In fact perfect pilgrimages were made to Carl, who always received the pilgrims with pleasant words and cheerful smiles. Carl was not insensible to the pleasure he derived from being able in turn to present to Magde the gifts he received from his friends.

"Ah," Nanna often said, "how pleasant it is to be beloved," and she would sigh as she thought of the absent one who had vowed to love her forever, and whose word was her creed of life. How much happiness Nanna derived from this creed! It solaced her in many lonely hours, and produced a favorable effect upon her every action and thought. She no longer was oppressed, as formerly, with dreaming indolence. Her cheeks were roses now.

Old Mr. Lonner and Magde were much gratified at this unexpected change in Nanna's deportment, and they could account for it only by supposing that she was much wiser than other girls of her age.

Carl, however, had peculiar views upon this subject, and when Nanna would exclaim, "O, how pleasant it is to be beloved!" he would reply:

"You know right well that there is some one who loves you, or else you would not be so light hearted."

When Carl thus spoke Nanna would blush with confusion.

"You must not speak so when any one can hear you," she would reply.

Carl would then nod his head pleasantly, and one day he

learned the secret, for he felt he could not remain long on this earth, and he wished to know all, and aside from that Nanna was anxious to discover whether he believed as firmly as she did in Gottlieb's vows.

"Do you think, Carl," said she, as she concluded her recital, "do you think he will return?"

"As certainly as I shall never see the sun rise on St. John's day, for I saw that in his eye, which assured me he would not break his promises."

"Why do you use such an ominous comparison, Carl? Why do you think you will not see the sunrise on St. John's day?"

The pain caused by the beginning of Carl's remark, clouded the pure joy which his concluding words would have otherwise created.

"I am waiting," said he, "only that I may see the lilacs bloom once more. In those beautiful flowers I have found my greatest joy."

Old Mr. Lonner occasionally attempted to prepare his son's mind for the future which awaited him; but he ceased when one day Carl innocently addressed him:

"Father," said he, "I wish you would not talk with me thus. I believe in our Saviour and his love for us sinners, and as I do not think I have done much harm - except perhaps when I stole the game - I fear not for the future. I shall wait patiently until my Saviour chooses to take me to himself. I can well imagine that there is not much space in heaven; but I believe that there is a small place for one so insignificant as me, where I can wait the coming of Magde, Nanna, Father, Ragnar, and all the little ones, that is if they do not hold me in contempt."

"How strangely you talk, dear Carl!" said Magde, entering into the conversation. "You well know that I would like to be near you in heaven, for you are aware that next to Ragnar I love you more than any other being on earth."

"You say so only to make me happy; but I am not so vain as to believe your words."

"Is there any one here who displays more love for you than I?" inquired Magde.

Carl smiled, and glanced at the wall. There hung a new vest, the pattern of which Carl examined as carefully as though each thread had been a painting in itself.

"Do you think," said he, after a pause, during which his father left the room, "do you think that Ragnar is vexed with me? He certainly must have observed that I love you more than, perhaps, I should - I speak frankly to you, Magde, for I know you are different from others, and I could not die in peace if I thought that my brother Ragnar was offended with me."

"Be convinced, my dear Carl, that Ragnar loves you as a brother should. He saw undoubtedly that no one could please you so well as I; but he often told me, and especially before his last departure - "

"What did he say?" inquired Carl, eagerly.

"'Magde,' said he, 'never desert Carl. He is an honest and faithful soul, who can find no joy unless with you; but Carl is not the one who would seek to injure me by word or thought, and therefore I shall not interfere with his sentiments, but allow him to entertain them freely, and,' he added, 'you may tell him this at some future time when he may feel troubled on my account.'"

"Did he speak thus, assuredly?"

"He did, I swear it by my hopes of meeting him again."

Emilie F. Carlen

"And you have obeyed him, and not deserted me; but will you do so as long as I am with you here?"

"Never shall I desert you, Carl."

"And when the last moment approaches," said he in a soft tone, "you will moisten my lips, you will smooth my pillow, and when the struggle of death comes upon me, I wish you to hold my hand in yours, as you now do, that I may feel that you are with me. Then you must - will you do so, Magde? - close my eyes with your own hands, and sing a psalm to me."

To all these touching requests, which were rendered still more affecting by the tender expression of his eyes, Magde replied tearfully:

"My dear Carl, your words shall be obeyed."

Carl smiled. He was now happier at the thought of his approaching death, which would bring such proofs of Magde's affection, than one who might have possessed a prospect of a long and luxurious life.

The lilac bushes blossomed, and Magde placed the first flowers in his hands while he yet could inhale their fragrance. The last flowers she strewed upon his grave.

CHAPTER XX

CONCLUSION

A long season of gloom and despondency succeeded the death of Carl.

It was fortunate that Ragnar returned home at an earlier period than usually; the flowers on Carl's grave had not withered when Magde piously conducted him to his brother's final resting-place.

"Rest in peace, poor brother," said Ragnar, brushing away a tear, "God saw best to take you from us - but, dear Magde, you must not grieve too much for his death, or you will not be able to rejoice at the news I have for you."

"What news, Ragnar?"

"Captain Hanson, who has been master of the brig Sarah Christiana ever since I have been her mate, has latterly become very much reduced in health, and he has concluded not to go to sea again."

"Well, that cannot be joyful news. He was a better captain than perhaps you will ever sail under again."

"I shall never sail under another captain. I shall be captain myself, hereafter. The owners of the vessel have tendered the captaincy to me."

"Is it possible?"

"It will soon be more than possible, for my old captain has so well recommended me, that Mr. Lund has advanced me a sufficient sum of money to pay the charges of my examination, and as soon as Christmas is over - for until then I shall study at home - I will take a journey to prepare myself, and after the examination you will be the wife of a captain. Then you and Nanna can go with me to Goteborg, that you may see the vessel before I go to sea."

Magde quietly clasped her hands. Her pious gratitude was evinced in her every expression. She thanked her God for having thus favored them with fortune.

Ragnar silently embraced her. "I did not say anything about it yesterday, for I wished to tell you here near Carl, who always placed his pleasures aside that they might not interfere with yours."

"Bless you, bless you, Ragnar! I now know why I found so many four leaved clovers last summer - only think, a captain's wife! - and still you love me as before?"

"Now and forever, my Magde. You shall have a bonnet as magnificent as any other lady; you shall have a cashmere shawl, and a black silk dress. Yes, I promise you all this, and more."

"Let us return home quickly, that I may rejoice father and Nanna."

And Nanna and her father were as much rejoiced at the glad tidings as was Magde herself.

A few days afterwards, Magde and her father were seated together in the parlor consulting about the future.

"The Lord thus distributes joys and sorrows. One year ago our prospects were much different."

"Have I forgotten that time? No! And if I should live a hundred years, I would never forget the day you were taken from us to prison, nor the day you were released by Mr. Gottlieb. This year Ragnar must send him the balance still due him."

"We can repay him the money; but we can never reward him for his kindness and love. He has not returned to Almvik, and perhaps it is for the best, and as Nanna under any circumstance - "

The old man was suddenly interrupted by a shrill blast from the outside, which blast was produced by some one blowing upon a blade of grass.

"Well, well," exclaimed Magde glancing through the window, and then rushing to the door, "the old proverb is true, 'talk of - '"

"A certain gentleman and he is here," interrupted Gottlieb, entering the door with his face beaming with his usual cheerfulness. He presented one hand to Magde, and the other to old Mr. Lonner, who exclaimed with glistening eyes:

"Welcome, welcome, Mr. Gottlieb. Ragnar intended to write you to-day, and I just told Magde we are able to discharge one part of our debt, but the other can never be repaid."

"Enough, enough, good father Lonner, I too was influenced by a selfish motive - but pardon me, where is Nanna?"

"She has gone to fish with Ragnar and little Conrad," said Magde, who had already manufactured an urn of coffee, "but they will soon return."

"Aha! is Mate Lonner at home. Then I can become acquainted with him."

"*Captain* Lonner, next spring at least, Mr. Gottlieb," said

Magde, proudly.

"Crown Secretary, now, instead of Mr. Gottlieb, if you please, Mrs. Lonner."

"So soon?"

"Yes, eight days ago I received the appointment; but my *great* fortune will come next spring, for then I hope to have a little house of my own."

"Yes, and perhaps a housekeeper too," added Magde.

"Possibly."

At this reply Magde cast a secret glance towards her father, which he returned. Gottlieb, however, changed the conversation, and commenced speaking of the death of poor Carl of which he had before been informed. During the next half hour, Gottlieb evinced the utmost impatience. He would walk to the window and gaze anxiously towards the lake, not observing that Magde and her father were exchanging significant glances and smiles behind his back.

At length he spied the boat, and he hastened down to the beach. The skiff contained the brother and sister, and their little companion.

A sympathetic sentiment seemed to have pervaded the entire family, for during their excursion Nanna and Ragnar conversed almost entirely about her young friend Gottlieb. So nicely had Ragnar probed his sister's heart that he knew almost as much about its true condition as Carl had previously learned. Although Ragnar would have desired to have believed as Carl did, he did not think it proper to offer Nanna any further consolation, than by saying that since he had received a captaincy she was placed on a more equal footing with Gottlieb and that he would do everything in his power to render her happy.

"I know you will, Ragnar," replied Nanna, "but only one thing can ever afford me happiness."

After these words the conversation ceased, and the brother and sister commenced their homeward ride.

In his great haste Gottlieb nearly ran into the water, in which Ragnar was standing fastening the boat; but so much was he astonished by the marvellous change which taken place in Nanna's appearance that he was forced to start back and gaze silently upon her. Nanna in the meantime appeared abstracted. She had not observed Gottlieb's approach; but sat in the boat slowly moving one of the oars, apparently in the deepest thought.

But how can we describe Nanna's joyful surprise when she discovered Gottlieb. Ragnar's presence prevented her from giving vent to her joy in words; but the joyful expression of her eyes was a more than sufficient welcome.

We will not describe the first interview between Ragnar and Gottlieb - suffice it to say it was the meeting of two brothers; not of two strangers. Neither will we describe the first hour of *mutual* congratulations; but we will at once draw the reader's attention to a pleasing picture near the fountain in the meadow. Here the two lovers had proceeded that they might confer with each other uninterrupted.

"You see, my little nymph, I have come back. Do you think that I have an honorable spirit and a true heart? Now tell me, have you grown so beautiful, for me; yes so beautiful that I can well be proud of you as my own little wife?"

"Wife! are you then serious?"

"Serious we shall never be, we will make a third agreement, which is that we shall live henceforth without a gloomy thought or serious foreboding. Although we shall marry, as it is said, for 'love in a cottage,' yet we are both so familiar with the reality of the cottage, that our romantic dreams, if we have any, will be fully realized."

"True, very true," said Nanna smiling, and her countenance radiant with joy, appeared still more beautiful, "and now I am - "

" - Betrothed," said Gottlieb joyfully embracing her.

How happy were the inmates of the little cottage that evening!

* * * * *

When the news of Gottlieb's betrothal reached Almvik, Mrs. Ulrica foretold that nothing but evil would result from the wedding.

Mr. Fabian, however, who secretly esteemed Gottlieb, was silent; but afterwards when the young couple were firmly united he would hold them up as examples and say that some men could be happy with a wife who did not possess riches and station.

"But that," insisted Mrs. Ulrica, "is no reason why a poor man should not know to prize the happiness which a wealthy wife could procure for him."

Choose from Thousands of 1stWorldLibrary Classics By

Ada Leverson
Adolphus William Ward
Aesop
Agatha Christie
Alexander Aaronsohn
Alexander Kielland
Alexandre Dumas
Alfred Gatty
Alfred Ollivant
Alice Duer Miller
Alice Turner Curtis
Alice Dunbar
Ambrose Bierce
Amelia E. Barr
Andrew Lang
Andrew McFarland Davis
Andy Adams
Anna Sewell
Annie Besant
Annie Hamilton Donnell
Annie Payson Call
Annonaymous
Anton Chekhov
Arnold Bennett
Arthur Conan Doyle
Arthur M. Winfield
Arthur Ransome
Atticus
B.H. Baden-Powell
B. M. Bower
Baroness Emmuska Orczy
Baroness Orczy
Basil King
Bayard Taylor
Ben Macomber
Bertha Muzzy Bower
Bjornstjerne Bjornson
Booth Tarkington
Boyd Cable
Bram Stoker
C. Collodi
C. E. Orr
C. M. Ingleby
Carolyn Wells
Catherine Parr Traill
Charles A. Eastman
Charles Dickens
Charles Dudley Warner
Charles Farrar Browne

Charles Ives
Charles Kingsley
Charles Klein
Charles Lathrop Pack
Charles Whibley
Charles Willing Beale
Charlotte M. Braeme
Charlotte M. Yonge
Charlotte Perkins Stetson
Clair W. Hayes
Clarence Day Jr.
Clarence E. Mulford
Clemence Housman
Confucius
Cornelis DeWitt Wilcox
Cyril Burleigh
D. H. Lawrence
Daniel Defoe
David Garnett
Don Carlos Janes
Donald Keyhoe
Dorothy Kilner
Dougan Clark
Douglas Fairbanks
E. Nesbit
E.P.Roe
E. Phillips Oppenheim
Edgar Rice Burroughs
Edith Van Dyne
Edith Wharton
Edward J. O'Biren
Edward S. Ellis
Edwin L. Arnold
Eleanor Atkins
Eliot Gregory
Elizabeth Gaskell
Elizabeth McCracken
Elizabeth Von Arnim
Ellem Key
Emerson Hough
Emily Dickinson
Enid Bagnold
Enilor Macartney Lane
Erasmus W. Jones
Ernie Howard Pie
Ethel Turner
Ethel Watts Mumford
Eugenie Foa
Eugene Wood

Evelyn Everett-green
Everard Cotes
F. H. Cheley
F. J. Cross
Federick Austin Ogg
Ferdinand Ossendowski
Francis Bacon
Francis Darwin
Frances Hodgson Burnett
Frances Parkinson Keyes
Frank Gee Patchin
Frank Harris
Frank Jewett Mather
Frank L. Packard
Frank V. Webster
Frederic Stewart Isham
Frederick Trevor Hill
Frederick Winslow Taylor
Friedrich Kerst
Friedrich Nietzsche
Fyodor Dostoyevsky
G.A. Henty
G.K. Chesterton
Gabrielle E. Jackson
Garrett P. Serviss
Gaston Leroux
George Ade
Geroge Bernard Shaw
George Durston
George Ebers
George Eliot
George MacDonald
George Meredith
George Orwell
George Tucker
George W. Cable
George Wharton James
Gertrude Atherton
Grace E. King
Grace Gallatin
Grant Allen
Guillermo A. Sherwell
Gulielma Zollinger
Gustav Flaubert
H. A. Cody
H. B. Irving
H.C. Bailey
H. G. Wells
H. H. Munro

H. Irving Hancock	James DeMille	Louisa May Alcott
H. Rider Haggard	James Joyce	Lucy Fitch Perkins
H. W. C. Davis	James Lane Allen	Lucy Maud Montgomery
Hamilton Wright Mabie	James Lane Allen	Lydia Miller Middleton
Hans Christian Andersen	James Oliver Curwood	Lyndon Orr
Harold Avery	James Oppenheim	M. Corvus
Harold McGrath	James Otis	M. H. Adams
Harriet Beecher Stowe	James R. Driscoll	Margaret E. Sangster
Harry Houidini	Jane Austen	Margaret Vandercook
Helent Hunt Jackson	Jens Peter Jacobsen	Margret Penrose
Helen Nicolay	Jerome K. Jerome	Maria Edgeworth
Hendrik Conscience	John Burroughs	Maria Thompson Daviess
Hendy David Thoreau	John Cournos	Mariano Azuela
Henri Barbusse	John F. Kennedy	Marion Polk Angellotti
Henrik Ibsen	John Gay	Mark Overton
Henry Adams	John Glasworthy	Mark Twain
Henry Ford	John Habberton	Mary Austin
Henry Frost	John Joy Bell	Mary Catherine Crowley
Henry James	John Kendrick Bangs	Mary Cole
Henry Jones Ford	John Milton	Mary Hastings Bradley
Henry Seton Merriman	John Philip Sousa	Mary Roberts Rinehart
Henry W Longfellow	Jonas Lauritz Idemil Lie	Mary Rowlandson
Herbert A. Giles	Jonathan Swift	M. Wollstonecraft Shelley
Herbert N. Casson	Joseph A. Altsheler	Maud Lindsay
Herman Hesse	Joseph Carey	Max Beerbohm
Homer	Joseph Conrad	Myra Kelly
Honore De Balzac	Joseph E. Badger Jr	Nathaniel Hawthrone
Horace Walpole	Joseph Hergesheimer	Nicolo Machiavelli
Horatio Alger Jr.	Joseph Jacobs	O. F. Walton
Howard Pyle	Julian Hawthrone	Oscar Wilde
Howard R. Garis	Julies Vernes	Owen Johnson
Hugh Lofting	Justin Huntly McCarthy	P.G. Wodehouse
Hugh Walpole	Kakuzo Okakura	Paul and Mabel Thorne
Humphry Ward	Kenneth Grahame	Paul G. Tomlinson
Ian Maclaren	Kenneth McGaffey	Paul Severing
Inez Haynes Gillmore	Kate Langley Bosher	Percy Brebner
Irving Bacheller	Kate Langley Bosher	Peter B. Kyne
Israel Abrahams	Katherine Cecil Thurston	Plato
Ivan Turgenev	Katherine Stokes	R. Derby Holmes
J.G.Austin	L. A. Abbot	R. L. Stevenson
J. Henri Fabre	L. T. Meade	R. S. Ball
J. M. Barrie	L. Frank Baum	Rabindranath Tagore
J. Macdonald Oxley	Latta Griswold	Rahul Alvares
J. S. Fletcher	Laura Lee Hope	Ralph Henry Barbour
J. S. Knowles	Laurence Housman	Ralph Waldo Emmerson
J. Storer Clouston	Leo Tolstoy	Rene Descartes
Jack London	Leonid Andreyev	Rex Beach
Jacob Abbott	Lewis Carroll	Rex E. Beach
James Allen	Lilian Bell	Richard Harding Davis
James Andrews	Lloyd Osbourne	Richard Jefferies
James Baldwin	Louis Tracy	Richard Le Gallienne